A Small Dog Barking

BY THE SAME AUTHOR:

The Inanimate World (stories)
The Dreamlife of Bridges (novel)

A Small Dog Barking

« stories »

ROBERT STRANDQUIST

ANVIL PRESS | VANCOUVER | 2005

A Small Dog Barking
Copyright © 2005 by Robert Strandquist

All rights reserved. No part of this book may be reproduced by any means without the prior written permission of the publisher, with the exception of brief passages in reviews. Any request for photocopying or other reprographic copying of any part of this book must be directed in writing to ACCESS: The Canadian Copyright Licensing Agency, One Yonge Street, Suite 1900, Toronto, Ontario, Canada, M5E 1E5.

NATIONAL LIBRARY OF CANADA CATALOGUING IN PUBLICATION DATA

Library and Archives Canada Cataloguing in Publication

Strandquist, Robert Arthur, 1952-
    A small dog barking / Robert Strandquist.

ISBN 1-895636-69-8

    I. Title.

PS8587.T6789S63 2005   C813'.6   C2005-905449-2

Printed and bound in Canada
Cover design: Typesmith Design
Typesetting: HeimatHouse

Represented in Canada by the Literary Press Group
Distributed by the University of Toronto Press

The publisher gratefully acknowledges the financial assistance of the B.C. Arts Council, the Canada Council for the Arts, and the Book Publishing Industry Development Program (BPIDP) for their support of our publishing program.

Anvil Press Inc.
P.O. Box 3008, Main Post Office
Vancouver, B.C. V6B 3X5 CANADA
www.anvilpress.com

Contents

Dryer Sheets 7
Tents 15
A Small Dog Barking 27
Hamnet 31
Waiting for the Sky 63
The Shift 69
    1) A Bridge
    2) The Collectors
    3) The Way Station
Biggs and Little 103
Attack of the Fifty-Foot Man 111
The Piece 119
The Unbelonging 127
    1) The Gig
    2) Summer of Love
    3) Kitten
    4) The Five-Hundred-Year-Old Man

this book is for
Monsty

Dryer Sheets

Force, the inertial tugs and pulls a two-dimensional being experiences when he tries to walk a straight line in three-dimensional space —Riemann

Steve stood on the deck of his cabin and watched his dog, Sparks, loping through the tall grass, like a mythical sea, and the wide blue sky held but one small cloud. The dog drifted in a limitless freedom of being lost and held at the same time, a feeling reserved for dogs and young children.

He'd moved to the woods to escape the bad relationships, the flayed soul of city life. Dandelion killers had stolen the warm afternoons with their lawn mowers and weed-whackers. Dryer sheets, the scented ones, had killed the evening walk. No neighbourhood was free of it. Chemical rose, seamy lilac, unforgivable effrontery one and all. But their traces were leaving him slowly. Although potentially negative molecules had a way to haunt him too, getting in through some other slit in his fabric.

Was his memory so good, or was it an emotional heightening, a fear of dry-cleaners? His skin grew a fine hair of fear. His neighbours across the road were a quarter mile away. It was pretty much all crown land between him and Hundred Mile. He spit and tried to shake it, the disgust, like Sparks would. But Steve was no dog, and the smell was no false memory. Dryer sheets . . . out here?

He called Sparks and held the car door for him. They drove with the windows down trying to track the smell, stopping at crossroads, listening by a stream. Wasn't fabric soft enough? It was fabric; what could be softer than that?

That night Steve couldn't get them out of his head, the garden banshees, the edgers, the eaters, the rectifiers. The whole point of their being gardens, was about that, wasn't it? Balm for the soul? Why always this conquering of the innocence by mad inventors?

A long strip of grass passed under the oil pan as he drove up Jack's driveway. Two weeks ago he was over to buy a cord of firewood from the guy. He was supposed to deliver it by now. Was that his truck parked beside the mailbox, for sale?

Jack's partner, a Susan if ever he saw one, a long-limbed Virgo for sure, was in the woodlot, chopping. Two black labs ruminating at the head of the driveway came over to Sparks.

Hello . . . Steve called.

I saw you pulling in, she said, her voice squeaked, like she was out of practice.

Is Jack around?

Her washing was on a line, in close with a nice breeze. Reassuringly organic looking, no clockwork violets.

No, why? Jack's gone.

Is he selling his truck?

You got a truck? Her summer dress was like a breeze, colours worn thin, showy silhouettes as the light stole behind her.

No, just this. He indicated his Toyota. *Jack was going to deliver my cord.*

There's your cord, she said, pointing to a neatly stacked evenly split pile of fir.

He backed his car around and opened the hatchback.

This is going to take a few trips, he told her eyes.

Those intense eyes stayed with him for the rest of the afternoon, but he didn't mind. Steve was shooting arrows straight up and listening for how close they came down. Next day he made a few more trips, and Jack's pickup was looking more attractive. Jack was out of the picture, obviously something that was nobody's business but theirs.

By the time Steve had got half the cord moved he gave up. He drove over with Sparks to have a look at the truck.

He climbed into the cab, felt the relaxed embrace of a half-ton of this vintage—the seventies rocked. It had a cassette player and he wondered if it worked; roach clip in the glove box. He grabbed the For Sale sign off the windshield.

She was looking at a book when Steve and Sparks got out of the truck.

Reading poems? he asked.

Some men would rather be trees, she said. *A line from my book.*

And some would rather not be trees, he retorted coyly, *a line from my head.* He was attracted to the literary turn in this woman.

I don't know how much that old truck is worth, she told him when he handed her the sign. *How much do you think?*

Your beauty seems to come out of nowhere, he said, as though remembering lines he'd read, *in the vicinity of a streak of lightning.*

I don't recognize the . . .

I could see my way clear to . . . a couple . . .

Can I offer you something to drink, Mister . . .

Tea . . . would be fine. Real tea. Steve . . .

He told her he hated raspberry tea, which made them both laugh. He looked around the trailer, examined a few of her trinkets: little skulls, a squirrel, a mouse, a fox. They sat in silence for a bit, their cups cooling.

You have beautiful lips, Steve Tea.

What was left of the afternoon's sun traced the edge of her lace curtain like a welding torch.

The autumn days went belly up. The lakes froze over and Steve got his fishing rod out and bought some snowshoes and went up the road where no cars had been for a while. In summer, Emerald Lake was a spectacular mirror; now it just waited for spring.

He followed a trail Jack once told him about, to one of his best fishing spots. He chopped a hole in the ice and got down on his hands to clear away the tinkling fragments. He noticed a face under the surface. It was Jack's face, staring up at him like the missing link, his eyes strangely active.

Obligation, heaviness. A discovery which was not apparently unexpected, Jack having been reported missing months ago. It was reported that the police hadn't ruled out foul play, but no arrests were, as yet, being considered.

Steve scribed the geography of his base log onto the next one, log number two, as dictated by his elbows and abdomen and aching thighs, trying to keep the bubble in the level zone and the pencil on the wood. He hewed and heaved with an anxious saw at the excess between the lines, working in the chink of a temporary brace of two-by-fours. But he was just making it worse with each adjustment, the original cut that wasn't so bad. All he wanted was to make a porch. For the time being he would put up a blue tarp. He fastened it admirably snug with bungee cords.

A moist hardness absorbed the dirt and oil from his hands as he whittled away a sapling's bark, made it feel dry and not so naked and like two staffs, one inside the other. He passed it from hand to hand as he hiked the hills. When he leaned on it with both hands, the bear bell was silenced. The shallow valley gathering sound, raven proofs, snatches of traffic, a slow train accumulating below hearing, surfacing briefly to whistle.

A grey owl landed on a branch right in his line of vision, on a tree about a hundred yards away, and to keep it there, to not lose its pattern against the grey background, he let the world wink into the periphery instead of his attention.

Further into the valley, he came upon an artesian well. It looked almost human the way it assertively arched away from its source, reaching for something it couldn't afford, like the restlessness of glass, knowing its first step will be the last.

Every undulation here is distinct, yet every gully alike. He was thinking it would be easy to get lost on this swelling sea of landforms. He stared at the compass he'd wired to his staff as Sparks looked at him to discriminate his doggy fears. But he couldn't make it point back to the cabin. North was all well and good. But there was one for maps, one for compasses, one for the consciousness of satellites. Was a fourth north undiscovered still?

Steve could see the forestry station's antenna on the lookout and he climbed up there. The interior plateau spread around him, splayed out in all its rawness. The air was so clean, so clear he could see the Coast Mountains and the Rockies silhouetted in a distant mist. It was an edgeless shimmer of green.

Coming down off the summit, he came upon the widow's place from the back. Sparks ran ahead to meet the dogs. She was sitting on her porch when he came out of the trees. He hadn't spoken to her since the discovery, but as smoke had continued to circle her hill he assumed everything was okay, that she just needed some time to herself. After the humiliating experience of driving Jack's truck into town to report finding Jack's body to the police Steve needed a little time as well.

She stood up against her railing, and she was as beautiful as ever. *Would you drive me into town?* she asked, before he had a chance to say hello. And she was just as free-spirited and trusting as ever.

I was just cutting through . . . I actually got lost up . . . but I saw my blue . . . sure, okay.

He ran to his place, leaving Sparks with the black labs. He came back with the truck and drove her in, following her directions down one street and another. He waited while she went into the funeral home. She got back in with a package, a box. She wanted to go to the supermarket so he drove her there and waited for another half an hour with the box on the seat beside him.

When she got back with bags of groceries he caught an immediate whiff of some poison—some soap or perfume.

What's that smell? He was feeling his throat tighten.

What? Jack's ashes?

No, that chemical smell.

He goes through her bags.

What have you got in there, dryer sheets?

What do you take me for? She didn't like his tone.

He dropped her off and Sparks jumped in and they went home. He smoked a joint and lit a fire in the pit. He was angry, but he was free, sitting out under the stars. His shirt stank, but so what? Sparks was beside him. He stank too. Maybe he'd call her in the morning. A train was coming and he was on the tracks. He would have to stay away. He would *not* call her, period. He wondered what she was up to, with those lovely strong hands. Maybe she was in the woodlot, or washing clothes. Why was he not free of this? What was so important about pussy? The word *relationship* flickered through his mind. He felt his skin flare over with a borealis of fear.

Tents

Into Luxembourg I came, dragging a lonely life behind me like a parachute prematurely deployed. I was fed up with the business of tents and I was fed up with my family. Ever since the old man died and left us the company—and regrettably little genetic business sense—my siblings and I have been flailing. *You can't push a river* was what the old man liked to say, confident he'd said it all. But moulded by homilies and the indistinct form of instant shelter, the temporary cities we erected hung like washing on the line. The elemental forces of commerce would have blown us away long ago, except for one remarkable demand and the deepest pockets in the world.

I told them no more army contracts and that this job was to be my last. And I only agreed to this one because a fashion show seemed as good a swan song as any.

It was a trade show like all trade shows, a Mardi Gras without the fun, a hive of hustlers and hangers-on, the beautiful and the desperate, neither of which had much use for me. The peacock with the haunted mouth, the struck-match redhead, I only felt lonely around them, like somebody's dodgy uncle, playing pocket pool.

Walking to the site from my hotel I found the morning wanting. Old memories hooked into my skin and I noticed the years had lost no time putting distance between me and my loves, all still too vivid in my mind; me watching them go down, waving obliviously from the shore.

My sister Cleo called a staff meeting for my convenience, a bad sign. Fredrick was on his way from Kuwait where he was staring down the barrel of another sandstorm. Cleo had brought me a silk jacket from Paris and encouraged me to meet one of the models, thinking a woman would necessitate my continuing to work. She liked to intervene, believed inherited wealth obligated certain conventions, arbitrary beauties. She thought I'd be easier to manipulate if I would live up to her standards. To go with the jacket my brother Fredrick bought me some expensive shoes. It was too smooth, this society, too well greased for chance encounters to occur. Intuition had been cured, embarrassment stamped out, which left the complicated business of happenstance up to our own resources. I was considering going back to my room for my jeans and work boots, but I stopped in the site office to use the can. I just needed a few minutes of quiet.

I found myself staring at the mirror as I peed. I looked like a freak. That morning I had shaven off my beard and it was too much, too much of a change, too much face.

The office phone started chirping and I felt the old dread of countdowns, daydreams of waiting for the axe to fall.

No one of my staff was there to answer it. A cup of coffee sat steaming on a desk. The swivel chair was warm.

Habitech Industries. I answered, trying to sound professional, or at least not too depressed.

I had a woman's voice on the line, appealing to me in a distressed form of English, much that wasn't intended and nothing I could understand. A picture sprang to mind of a tall chestnut-haired woman, a Russian or a Pole. Her strange music soothed and delighted me and I tried to keep her talking, but she was no fool and dropped the phone in the busy air. I had to laugh. I could hear where she was calling from. I felt slighted, but I was charmed and I thought I'd better go and have a look.

Okay, everyone, back to work, I, the reluctant authority, pushing my way through hostile elbow territory, seeing for myself what the fuss was about: a hole in the tent connected to the main pavilion that the models used as a dressing room, a whole missing panel.

When I looked in it was like a fish tank, a medium of brightness and injured feelings awash in undergarments and suspended in a substance you could only describe as fluid.

I went round and showed my pass, made my way through the clouds of talcum dust, past strange skinny beings changing wherever they could.

I made my way to the side missing the panel and waited there while the Peeping Toms disengaged one by one, feeling like an idiot, until the supervisor got there with the materials to fix the problem. Then I searched the women's faces, wondering which one belonged to the voice on the phone. Once I'd separated the giraffes from the hyenas I spotted her, a petite brunette, beguilingly ordinary. Her lopsided syntax within these waylays created its own reality. Spinning it from silk and peach fuzz, pinning and underpinnings, a torn stocking, a busted clasp, a case of the jitters, dispatched with emotive fingers and a mouthful of pins, sending them, one by one, out onto the runway.

I only wanted to ask you . . . I managed to get her attention.

She shrugged at me as if to say *Can't you see my hands are full and I don't have time to congratulate you for doing your job.* But in her eye I saw more, the freed-slave look, the not knowing if she could trust herself, the not knowing if she could afford not to.

What was your name?

She took out the pins and said, *Marie.*

Mara, I said, affectionately rewriting her. *Did you mean to release my soul from its jar?*

I couldn't believe I'd said that. I was a madman when it came to women. What I meant to say was, *How about lunch sometime?* She was quiet for a moment, her lips interviewing her thoughts.

Marie, she stressed.

I was presumptuous. I apologized. *I'm getting in your way . . .*

Later I followed her to a restaurant. She got a table off to herself and held a conversation with the stillness and smoked a cigarette. I found a corner nearby and had the waiter deliver a rose to her table but, like a fibre floating from my hand, she was already gone.

For the rest of the afternoon I watched her through the long end of the day, caught her in ambiguous silhouettes moving over the inside of the tent.

The next morning I met Cleo and Fredrick at my brother's hotel. He had rented a small conference room that was too big for the three of us. We sat around tables pushed together in a square and looked at each other across the wood grain.

What is it? Cleo asked me, cutting to the chase.

Frankly, I'm fed up, I told them.

No, I mean, what's different about you?

Can't you tell? Fredrick said, with a snide smirk barely hidden by his own moustache and goatee.

Your beard . . . Cleo clued in. *Oh, god, please . . .*

Don't make the poor guy feel bad . . . Fredrick was pouring himself a drink.

Well, it's just that he looks so . . .

He knows, he knows, shut up about it already.

It was your idea, I told Cleo. *About shaving off my beard.*

Don't be absurd.

To change the subject, Fredrick asked me, *Have you met any women, any of the models?*

As a matter of fact—
Our mother could have been a model, Cleo mused.
How do you know that? Fredrick asked.
From her picture.
You can't tell something like that from one picture . . .
She was *tall enough.*
Do all models have to be tall?

Cleo turned back to me. *You should have kept the beard. That's all I'm saying. It's like I'm talking to a stranger.*

Maybe you are, I told her.

It softened your . . . it hid the family mouth.

The old man had one thin set of lips, Fredrick said sadly.

Our father had been killed by the wind. It ran him through with a piece of aluminum bracing.

Fredrick was trying to make a point about why I owed them another year before I "fucked off," as he put it. He said things were going rather too well to start slacking off now. Cleo lit a cigar and put her feet up on the table.

There is such a thing as family loyalty, she said.

By the time the meeting was over I wasn't myself. Unable to justify my long silences to their satisfaction, I left feeling ruined, their voices stuck in my neck. They took my refusals to mean that I agreed to disagree. They wanted just one more year. Cleo scheduled another meeting for the next day and told Fredrick not to let me out of his sight. Everything had taken on a pallor of madness.

I needed to grab hold of something for support and thought of

Marie. I bought a bouquet of carnations and went to find her. She was all I had, one thin thread to pull me back from this. Nothing from my past came forward to support me. It was the last day of the show and I was afraid of missing her. I was nearly running, breathing premonitions of loss. When she emerged from the pavilion I could see she was looking for me, and when I saw the relief spread across her face I knew she was mine.

And that's when Fredrick showed up and started browbeating me over Bosnia. I could just imagine what Marie was thinking, as I slipped sideways into the black ditch of family emotions. Fredrick on his knees begging me not to abandon them with things going so well. That's when Marie made one of those bird-swift escapes, but not before she uttered a last word; though I couldn't catch it, I read it on her lips: *Milan . . .*

•

Armies run on tents, regardless of what else you've heard. This was Cleo's philosophy, about everything pretty much. We were already a rich family and these peace missions were taking us someplace else altogether. Every hour was tight with interest, every accident littered with disembodied gold. Our caravans of trucks overcame the inconstant sands, supplying the endless bracing, the miles of nylon, replacement crews for the replacement crews. Cleo held us together with her hypnotist plagues, requiring of family loyalties that were completely incredible, an inexorable dance to the world's cheapest violin. One location became another, though always in the narrows of an hourglass your compassion for time wore raw in the sand. Night poured into day over Egypt, and the Nile snaked in for a closer look.

We created small cities next to the curious river and I worked out my anger. Our structures blossomed like shingles on a young girl's skin, to the dull music of aluminum jamming and the howling of incurable things. I'd drive out at dusk and find a dune, let the sun paint my face red while I watched the river roll and lengthen and curl, queen of infamy, taboo of taboos. Sometimes I thought she was looking right at me, and I'd contemplate orgasm by drowning. But after the sun went out I grew cold from thinking too much, stuck on recombinant photographs of old wombs, about the black Nile and how perfectly she fit her image of herself.

I had let my beard grow back and taken up smoking as a way to remember what might have been, the one important moment we are doomed to repeat in perpetuity. Like the old refrain about humans being better than animals, like the fifty-seven words for resentment, the restless rasp of the ibis bird.

Yah, life was cheap. The last of the sun's daggers went in and died beautifully. Reduced to subtext, the moon shivered over an alien room.

My crews were manned by gamblers and husbands with ironclad misconceptions about the age they were running from. Focused on putting a stake together or paying off some long forgotten hood, they were prisoners of a ringing in the ears. Only the rich knew how worthless money really was.

One night while the men watched a video, a cheap porn flick, I saw a hand come out of the ground. It was less than tangible, more than air. Like tacit steam rising from the earth, a hyper nothing, it lifted one of the men up and held him above the ground for a few seconds, like it was showing off. The old boy screamed in a way that seemed more ecstasy than terror. Then it dropped him onto the folding chairs and a strange feminine scent lingered for hours afterwards.

A couple of prostitutes found their way into camp and the party went on late into the night. I tried to sleep, regardless, and at one point went outside to stretch and piss and noticed something was missing. The mess tent was missing. It was gone.

I grabbed my flashlight and followed the marks in the sand where the huge tent had been dragged off. I ran back and fired up the generator and aimed a propane spotlight over the dunes. I got in my Jeep and followed the tracks down to the river. Then I found I was swimming—minutes later, hours later, I didn't know—far out from shore. I don't know how far down they pulled me out.

You're starting to scare us, my sister told me, surrounding me with her presence in my hospital room. Days had gone missing. I was laid up for an infection in my shoulder. Something jagged in the riverbank had snagged me as I crawled out. A medical team had been dispatched to the spot to locate it. The infection was serious and unknown, but it healed eventually, though in certain kinds of weather it produced a throbbing pain, and occasionally an agony that I got lost in.

When I told Cleo I wanted the Milan fashion show contract, she looked at me for a moment. She leaned on the back legs of the hospital's chair and butterflied her elbows. She was picking up the scent of something.

I thought you were free of that . . . seamstress.

I said nothing.

You don't want to do an arms show? she asked.

I told you . . .

Cleo was amused and affronted by everything, not just me. She was looking at my face, at the hairless family lip. But I had to shave if Marie was going to recognize me. If I was right about Milan, if I was able to find her.

The city wasn't famous for its rain, but it was pouring that week. All the models looked damp, the tents were slick. I stood on the brink of a tarp and smoked, thinking of nothing, blowing rings, watching it come down. What I liked about smoking was that it gave you something to do.

The past year had been a waste, but I kept thinking about the incident with the missing panel, sucking on imagination's bitter milk, making myself weak. My injured shoulder pulled at my affections, and I realized that the rain wasn't rain; it was she, the Nile, Alexandria, that she had followed me here.

Then I spotted Marie, between the pavilions in a slicker, looking different—her hair or something—and tired, tangled up in coat hangers. I drew a breath and lost my courage. Did I belong in another place and time?

I was trying to think, but it was like trying to light a cigarette in the rain.

She looked up and I could see she was pleased, surprised and not surprised. I tossed the soggy end.

Look at you, you're soaked. You should have a hat, I told her.

No . . . is something in the rain, she said, and brushed something from my shoulder.

It was enough.

A Small Dog Barking

Mete had noticed bar codes appearing on things long before the scanners appeared in the stores. In prison he tried to make the connection, but the iceberg it was the tip of floated just out of reach. In jail you live in your head, but Mete had always lived in his head. Jail wasn't a big change. He tried to make the connections but there were none. Church was a conspiracy to keep you from God. Families ensured you never had intimacy with anyone. Justice, a jury of your peers, just one more extinction event. Lazarus raised from the dead should not be in charge of the nursery.

One night the wrath of God trampled all over his imitation Persian rug, breaking several of his fingers, landing him in a cell where he was immediately raped by a chalk outline. Jail was where you were force-fed time. The biggest thing that never existed, they pushed it down your throat. It was all you had to think about, that and your crime, if you were lucky enough to have one. In the early days family visited, bringing their baskets of memories. As their visits became more strained, they wanted him to confess to the poor woman's murder. They were tired of making the trip, but naturally they denied it. Mete was glad when they stopped coming. It was like when everyone knows something they're not telling you, something they know about you, something too appalling to tell you about yourself. Tidy resolutions, adherence to irrefutable absurdities.

Just remember to take cell doors at a crouch, and the chairs kill your back if you try and relax in them, all the while trying to block the clatter out, elbowing suspicious bowls of meal. Everywhere, propaganda proclaimed that revenge had been eradicated from the face of the earth, but they never told you about the vial they'd lost somewhere in the files.

Already one parole hearing was a file folder; his test score grid didn't line up to the machine's, so they turned him down. When they told him, he just nodded like they made all the sense in the world, relaxing his muscles, taking it in. The warden had to placate the guards' union, the government mandarins, the news media, his wife. Somebody had to pay for it all.

DNA was no sooner coined when it turned up in forensics. He could see it coming and then it overtook him, like bar codes. Ambitious smalls were always making everything smaller; it was the great stone, the great uphill. What occurred occurred because of the completely unrelated connections between things. It was the warden, claiming rashly, in public, that no wrongly accused men were being held in his facility.

It was the urine sample of fate, a piece of meat on the head of a pin. Some pinching and probing, and a few tests and sword dances later, the odds were in his favour, ranging in the billions to one. The DNA tests were conclusive and the warden was out on his ass, but it took months before Mete staggered down into the valley a free man. There had been no hoopla, nobody on the outside waving in. City administration threatened him and lawyers shouted. A priest whispered that he should forgive God. And the only free shrink found him repellent.

He rented a room in his old neighbourhood and relaxed in his gonch. What it was simply went on. The public found his vague innocence troubling. Slowly he resigned himself to the traumas in the walls and the not insignificant reigns of garbage. It didn't matter; he'd become an old madman long ago, anyway.

One night after he'd turned out his lamp it all started again. He thought he was having a dream: his door flying open, six Navy seals framing him in watertight pistols. They called him a *terrorist motherfucker,* bound his wrists with zap-straps and were about to drag him down the stairs when a bright light in the crowd realized they were in the wrong room, on the wrong floor. This revelation was followed by a considerable pause. One of them reluctantly reached out with his bayonet and, with a flick, cut the zap-strap. Covering each other, they withdrew. A minute later there was a crash on the floor below, a cry of protest cut short. A small dog barking.

Hamnet

*Let me speak to the yet
unknowing world how these
things came about.*
—Horatio

It was the only thing on for days, solemn and strange, the black veil, blurry Hamnet saluting the horses that pulled his father's giant casket, all wrapped up like a present, a wedding present. It was the beginning of his remembered life, that moment his mother's fingers brushed his cheek told him all there was to know. The years unfolded like a map of the world, with its pubic scrawl of lines curling back, its roads abruptly terminating at the edge; the needs of a woman, independent of her son, where whole unexplored regions were coloured pink, deplete of roads or towns or rivers. After all they'd been through, after all that, this. Hamnet was giving her away. To some patient cod, standing there waiting beside a pillar that dwarfed him and the Bishop standing beside him. He met Hamnet's coal stare, gloomy and fond. The shape of every syllable ever whispered now bathed in echo—this was Hamnet's procession down the aisle, his mother on his arm.

Gertrude whispering, *Dwarfed by the architecture, see how insignificant a man is.*

One tiresome bar after another, the music of going along. That blessed organ, surrounded by a Christ of lead and glass where you could hear a pin drop but not a word of what was being said. Crouched in the translucent air, a city wears its cathedral like a crown, its chiseled lace floating on the hill like a shaft of light.

When they got to the altar, the groom leaned in and whispered to Hamnet, *Do you mind if I call you son?*

There were better places Hamnet could be. Sifting for his father's profile in the dust behind a filing cabinet at the archives, feeling for the predicate still beating under a shredder somewhere. An official report was its own smoking gun, but disbelief never was enshrined as a right.

Let me get back to you on that, was his cool reply.

Eduardo Federico didn't react to Hamnet's slights. He was a supporter of angry young men, and saw potential in this one. His sons stood with him on the other side of the generation gap, beckoning to their own sons. But it was hard to raise a man. Undermined by the social solvents of lassitude and praise, they were attracted to whatever element found them first.

Hamnet and I flew out together a week later, to the reception in Spain. I was looking forward to seeing the estate. It was said to hold several climates within its boundaries, and to give onto the Mediterranean like a beautiful naked woman. This was Eduardo's aside to me, when he invited, nay, begged me, to accompany Hamnet over. I tried to cheer him up, but my jokes were stale, something was eating him. If ever a person deserved to feel good about themselves it was Hamnet. But when I suggested as much by way of encouragement, his face just darkened.

The reception dawned in glorious sunshine and I was comfortably ensconced in the situation. Colourful tents and tarpaulin canopies provided shade. There was a wedding cake as high as a stalk of corn, all decked out in appalling sugar roses of horrid pink and yellow icing and, of course, a well-stocked bar.

Weddings . . . Hamnet sighed.

Humiliating and ridiculous to any whole man, I replied.

Degrading and stultifying.

The worst of it is the complicity of your friends.

What is a bride if not a piece of propaganda?

A poor substitute for an inner life.

A landscape of thorns.

Death by cookie-cutter.

If I ever defeats the gun lobby, Hamnet mused, closing one eye like Popeye, *I'll t'oyn my sights on weddings.*

He did the characteristic chuckle and we went to the bar.

Two double scotches, I told the guy.

Gertrude's dress flickered like a school of gold fish, the way she moved. Exchanging authors with actors and old soldiers' wives, all of them floating in the same illusionist's medium, her chameleon hands, the groom's security mingled with the bride's people—*Hey, Rocky, watch me pull a rabbit out of my hat!*—I handed him his drink.

Eduardo was nearby and engaged in a conversation with one of his nieces, teaching her about wine, encouraging her past the initial bitterness.

The Princedoms of Gob, I said, in relation to my thoughts, and to get a response from my friend. But he wasn't listening to me.

Do you think giving her liquor is such a good idea? Hamnet asked the older man.

Liquor? Eduardo looked up, searched his memory for a translation of the word. *You speak but you do not speak. There is technically no word for what wine is.*

She's just a child. Hamnet was appalled and bemused.

Childhood is an illusion, Eduardo told him.

What if you're creating little drunkards?

Then Christ will favour her.

He's such a romantic . . . Hamnet said looking at me.

Eduardo changed the subject, *See that man out there?* Pointing to a white suit next to Gertrude. *He says how you'd make a good candidate for your senate, no?*

Strike three. Hamnet ducked the reassuring hand. He'd been down the hall of uncles before. They touched your elbow or squeezed your shoulder, but didn't give you room. Fear of a child's questions made them impotent and stupid: What makes the sky blue? They were a vibration through the wall, counting backwards waiting for sleep. They all seemed too willing to reduce the legacy of Hamnet's father to a war-cry for money. Reduced to an unphotogenic detail, it underestimated out of all proportion: the choice Fortinbras stuck him with, sending two letters, the one hard and threatening, the other conciliatory. Fortinbras was inconsistent and dangerous, but he was a man, and, as such, didn't know how to proceed. Amidst a thunderstorm of voices he kept his own council, found a way to be simple.

Hamnet wandered over the secluded slopes, miserable, his emotions like grounded kites, waiting for a mood swing. He felt the cooked earth and tasted the sea salt breeze carried to him as if on a silver platter. Why could he not savour it, relish awareness of simple things? Instead he obsessed, something he'd read about on the plane over, an article about north, about there being a third north. There used to be just true north and magnetic north but now there was a new one, geometric north, what satellites got their bead on, a spot coinciding with the centre of the earth. While the emotional north, the one men orbited, seemed to always be shifting. It made him an easy target for the blues.

He came over a hill and found a young woman, one of the young moths unwittingly released into his path. She was holding a little sailboat, her posture unselfconscious, silhouetted against the horizontal sea. They played together as children.

Ophelia, he said, recalling a name.

Embarrassed, being caught at her thoughts, she frowned and offered him the toy boat.

Didn't we used to play strip poker, he asked, innocently enough, *under my mother's porch?*

You must be thinking of someone else.

Ophelia's parents were part of Gertrude's crowd, but a lower strata of her society, which made it easier for Hamnet to feel superior, and in a sense more at ease, freer to act out. But then, they were only children.

It's the only game I know, he laughed, *where the players want to lose.*

Why would they want to lose?

Come on, toss the boat on the ground, take my hand, can you climb?

They climbed a goat trail to a lookout. From there they could see the tents of the reception and how the sun stretched the guests into complacent shadows. Anyone looking up might have observed them.

You did lose as I recall, Ophelia said.

I probably cheated.

I probably wanted you to.

I didn't bring any cards.

You could flip a coin.

Winner take all?

Loser.

Ophelia's dress slipped away like water. Hamnet had no time to undress. It was like falling out of a tree. To come he had to crane his neck to see who, if anyone, was watching. It left him defenceless, in the wrong, again alone with the vacuum of space—a peculiarity of the unprepared imagination, innocently bending the landscape before it.

When they rejoined the party, Ophelia's parents were waiting, more or less patiently. Noticing the dishevelled dress and bewildered mouth, they exchanged a curious fleeting look. When they saw who was with her they couldn't help but give it away. Gertrude was in a huddle with them, going over the particulars of the day in finer and finer detail. Ophelia went and sat with her brother, who was grim with boredom, in the back seat of their rented Citron.

I was sitting off to myself. I had borrowed Eduardo's binoculars. I'd had too many stressful encounters and was contemplating my drink. Hamnet sat down on the grass beside me. He'd been at his mother's purse, to her pills. He took one and replaced the top and tossed them to me. I don't know why he did that, and so casually. I tried to give them back but he was on his way someplace else. He looked at me rather cruelly and then laughed half apologetically, a complicated self-deprecating sound. I went to the can intending to drop them, but it felt pretty lame. So I took a few and sat back to catch the sun setting into the sea. Everything seemed to be lit from inside with its own soft glow.

After they made love, Ophelia huddled under his arm like a crutch. They had gained some skill as lovers since their experience on the hillside in Spain, but in a way it was still strip poker under his mother's porch. Physically he could only give and Ophelia was a good listener. An audience for all his different selves, it was all he really needed. I knew all about that particular role. But I was off to Wittenberg to study, so it didn't matter; and Hamnet, the good son, was following his mother's wishes into architecture. So be it.

Sometimes I find myself moving the pieces around, Hamnet says, sitting up.

How so? Ophelia on her elbow.

The patterns shift, he says, putting his pants on. *Logic goes a different direction.*

But isn't logic logical. I mean . . .

I know what you mean. You'd think so. But there's always a new face staring back.

You should make your move on these killers. How much more proof do you need?

Oh, they've laid their traps.

Isn't there anyone you can trust?

Define trust.

Friends . . .

Collaborators, opportunists.

Lover . . .

The catch, he told her, *in proving anything, is the mutual basis: the fact that you need one. The criminal has to agree that he's a criminal or else what have you got? Milosevic! Stalemate, the great victory.*

All's fair in love and war?
And who gave love such authority?
What have you got against love, my dear man?
It's not love I'm against, it's the word *love.*
What, that little drop?
I mean, can't a man only really love his . . .
What? His dog, his car?
Silly girl.

City University was in a world of its own on the seventieth floor of one of the tallest buildings in the world. It had a staff of venerable old secretaries and youngish professors who took pleasure in destroying at least one student a year. The talented ones seemed to raise the ire of the professors because they lacked something which neither could define—warmth. And success was not necessarily synonymous with talent. Hamnet explored the city, photographing the ostentatious and the simply crap to the grand and the grandioser. In bad light it all looked the same; monolithic errors and overwrought cheese graters, shit designed by mothers' sons who could just as easily have been pipe-fitters.

Aware that the driver had taken the wrong bridge, Hamnet looked at the man's baseball cap and smiled to himself. Did Hamnet look like an out-of-towner, wearing this shirt with palm trees that Ophelia had given him and a pair of virginally white runners she'd picked out as well?

Rather than complain to the taxi driver, he over-tipped the guy, to throw him off. Smug bastards, never give them anything. Hamnet went through the side gate into Gertrude's orchids. He found her on her knees in one of the beds.

Mother . . .

She sounded annoyed, *When are you going to learn to not be so irritatingly punctual?*

When am I going to learn to stay out of frivolous affairs? he came back with, ineffectually defending himself by leaving himself wide open.

She dropped the implement she was opening the ground with and wiped her forehead with the wristband of her glove.

There are no frivolous affairs, she said.

Do you like my shoes? he said to change the subject.

How was your class?

More arches and aqueducts.

Buildings are the Stonehenge of our time.

Yes, I know how you go into raptures over the Guggenheim.

There's nothing more fundamental.

Hamnet's instructors generally said the same kinds of things: draw the spaces around the object. Seemed like good advice. Hamnet could get his head around that, but never his hands, and that was the problem.

Bear Walk leaks, he said.

That's not possible.

Why?

Francis would not design a house that leaks.

I'm sure you're right. In fact, I was thinking of switching my major to acting.

She was being put in her place. He knew all the right buttons to push. But it said more to her than he knew; his attacks were, by default, weapons capable of producing anger, but which she could also just as easily deflect.

Is she the woman you want at your side? Gertrude asked, seriously, getting to the point.

Hamnet looked away. It was true, Ophelia was green, but she was more than just a friend.

Gertrude took off her sunhat and glanced at the shoes her son was wearing, but decided not to say anything. She took his arm and led him to the patio.

I'll get Gladys to make us tea.

Benjamin Houghton was the newest member of the faculty. He was famous in his field for experimental churches in the Persian Gulf, a ninety-storey cone in Norway, a whimsical toy block office complex precariously stacked on Hong Kong's docklands. His colleagues resented him and the students found his lectures esoteric and incomprehensible.

Because of Houghton's fear of heights he wouldn't go near the campus. Hamnet had to meet him at his office, which was in the basement of his firm, a non-descript two-storey block the great man had designed for himself.

Sit down, my boy.

Houghton leaned back on his chair and studied the face opposite him, apparently trying to stare him down.

Hamnet gazed back, unperturbed and slightly amused. He blinked first and looked around to take in the office. There was a large bookcase, several black and white pictures of skyscrapers, and, of course, no windows.

So, came Houghton's reassuring voice, very professorial, *what do you think of our noble profession?*

To be honest, Hamnet said, studying him, *I'm not sure.*

It hasn't caught you in its sway?

Hamnet smiled at the choice of words.

Maybe I just don't get it.

I see you brought your folder.

Yes, I have.

Hamnet unzipped the long sides of the folder. He didn't like showing his work to anyone and it was very painful when he didn't know how to read Houghton's mild surprise. He was flipping through the sheets with a noncommittal gleam, and only stopped to examine a group of photographs Hamnet had taken from around town, of gaudy bell towers and weather worn gargoyles, shots leering out over the city at sunset.

These are sincere.

Hamnet was perplexed by the comment, but grateful.

You disagree? Houghton inquired.

I don't know. It's hard to explain.

You belittling yourself with extraordinary care?

I just don't understand why buildings don't collapse under their own weight.

Houghton leaned back and studied the young man.

Let me ask you this . . . What makes a plane fly?

Wings?

Houghton laughed. *No,* he said, *not wings, gravity. Gravity is what allows a bird to fly, what makes a building stand.*

Ah. . .

It's a process called symmetry, the law of opposites.

Which law of opposites was that?

Houghton drummed his fingers on the leather arm of his chair.

Where are you when every step forward is a step back?

Hamnet stared, uneasy, longing to surrender to the man's charm, but wanting it to make sense.

Herodotus?

Hamnet's thoughts went suddenly back to the day a week earlier when he'd split up with Ophelia. The memory was a sinkhole, looking more and more like another mistake. The one he always made; the one where he trips himself up trying to please somebody else.

This thing you seek . . . what is it, revenge . . .

Evidence, Hamnet said. Was this man trying to use him? *What could you possibly know that I don't already know?*

Houghton nodded respectfully . . . *You'd be surprised.*

Ophelia had invited herself along on one of Hamnet's photography excursions, one he did regularly with a couple of buddies from school. They zoomed around the old neighbourhoods in Hamnet's convertible, parking in loading zones, backing down one-way streets, shadowing the illusive light. Ophelia was keeping a lookout for a patch of memorial lawn where she could spread a blanket and serve them lunch, chicken and cherries and white wine. Hamnet neglected to tell her that his friends were coming along, and this put a bit of a damper on the afternoon. They didn't see any point in carrying on after a couple hours and he dropped them off at City.

Hamnet and Ophelia attempted to resurrect her picnic under the miserable aspen in Gertrude's field, but it was Easter Sunday and the place was overrun with feral memories fanning out all over the yard. An all pervading jealousy seemed to hunt them. When Ophelia agreed to pose for Hamnet he tweaked her arms and tilted her neck at odd angles.

You're treating me like wire. And you're doing it on purpose.
Doing what?
Making me stupid.
Don't be an ass, he said.
What have I done?
What have you done?
Don't be cold.
Do you even know what the word means?
Cold? Yes, I think I know what the word means . . . Please, tell me what not to say and I won't say it. You don't know what it's like. My family's not like yours.

It had angered him, to see her so needy. Her words sounding

so prearranged and emotional. Like the smells coming off the garden reminded him of shopping malls. It was what he'd known all along.

I'm disgusted with myself for not ending this sooner.
You love me more than you know, she told him.
There'll be bitterness, I know.
I don't think you understand . . .
Ophelia's deflowering had become a public property.
A head on a plate . . . Houghton's voice pulled him back to the windowless present.
Hamnet looked around the office and at the man.
A head on a plate I cannot give you, but . . .
What can you—
First we need to put this unseemly business with the girl behind you.

And so he decided to get out of town for a while. In fact he would live with his mother and Eduardo on Eduardo's boat, spend the summer anchored in small ports around the Mediterranean basin.

He devoted his days to reading fiction and his nights trying to avoid Eduardo's crowd, occasionally getting trapped by some woman in some corner, bringing him face to face with his loneliness, to Ophelia, to missing her. The women he was meeting were interesting in ways, but always too . . . he couldn't pinpoint quite what. Distant? Living on a boat made it easier to keep it that way. For the time-being he was content to let summer expand into its corners. He was wanting for nothing and no thing was wanting for him.

About a month in, I showed up, rowing out in a dinghy I'd rented on the beach. I circled the yacht and called, trying not to tip. Hamnet appeared at the rail of this bobbing building. *Ship ho!* I yelled. *Landlubber off the stern. Hail Caesar* . . . I was feeling light-headed and a little careless. Hamnet stood at the ladder and took my arm as I climbed on deck.

Horatio! Is that really you?

I'm not sure . . . It's been a stressful day.

What are you doing out here? You haven't been sent into exile as well, have you?

The drugs, Hamnet, I told him candidly, still finding my sea legs, *And women. And I was in the neighbourhood. For old time's sake, and I'm here to spy on you, and besides, my firm suggested—insisted . . .*

You look like shit. Are you still in Norway?

No, Moscow now. I put in for it.

For what possible reason?

Do you know how hard it is to get pharmaceuticals there?

And that's a good thing?

I'm standing here, aren't I?

You'll never learn.

What am I supposed to learn?

How the fuck do I know? It's great to see you, even if you have come all this way to spy on me.

That evening we took the launch into town and had a leisurely tour of the outdoor cafés. In establishments strategically near the street we observed women walking. He'd changed, but what else was new? Much of what came out of his mouth was shit—not serious lies, just frictions, for effect, variations on themes that made the world more symmetrical. He bragged about one thing or another, but to me he just seemed kind of out of it.

A woman sat down at our table.

Here's my little Hamnet, she chimed, *with his broken heart, and a friend.*

She was dark gold, a bit of river. I introduced myself.

I want he should come for dinner. Only dinner. Tell him. We'll eat off the floor if he likes.

You dog, I told him.

You might think he's a dog, but he's a dog who only wants to be unlucky.

Poor boy . . .

He can't let go of something.

His heart has only three legs, I told her.

He pines away.

And I pee on the bushes, Hamnet said.

That's the difference, men pretend to love nobody, while we women pretend to love everybody. You see what I mean?

So you're saying Hamnet is pretending to pretend?

I'm saying he will have to do better than that. He could be a brilliant lover. Too brilliant.

But there are many fish in the sea. Hamnet was getting weary of the subject.

Are not many of these fish in your so-called sea, she said, *really just the first fish you happen to see?*

When we got back to the yacht, Eduardo was on the deck having a quiet drink, looking at the stars, so sad until we came on board, yet he concealed it. He looked like he was sick of the world. Hamnet barely acknowledged him and went below. I would have stayed but was too pissed not to make a fool of myself.

I fell onto my cot and lay on my back and thought about the first time I met Hamnet. It was in a play-making class, when we were shy little boys. It was a production built of scenes we children had written. Our teacher wove them into a narrative, used our bodies to construct props, rehearsed the paternal psychosis right out of us. Gertrude was there for the show, with a senator she was seeing at the time and some of her more obsequious friends. They took up the entire front row. The show came off well, Hamnet's vignette being the climactic story, something about slain dragons and being transformed.

In the morning we breakfasted on the aft deck with the continent gently lapping off the starboard. I was staring into my laptop. Hamnet was scanning the shore for a body that reminded him of Ophelia. Gertrude was studying him from under the rim of her hat.

Do you find European girls more refined? she asked her son.

They are like rocks, rocks that bleed, Eduardo offered the ensuing silence.

They understand the language of being with a man, Gertrude went on, fishing.

All women are women, Eduardo offered, as though to clear things up. *As all dragons are dragons.*

They have extraordinary minds and an unadorned beauty, I threw in, to remind them I was there.

They have extraordinary cunts, said Eduardo.

Gertrude was quiet for a moment. Eduardo winked at me like he'd won something. He moved the morning's devoured newspapers around on the deck with his feet.

What are your plans for next semester? Gertrude asked.

Without removing his gaze from the beach he said, *The municipality wants another museum, one with corners this time,* winking at Eduardo, sharing a private joke.

Whatever happened to the blonde? Eduardo asked. *She was built like a . . . how you say . . .*

A brick shithouse. Hamnet said.

A curious way for an architect to describe a woman, Gertrude moaned.

I'm no architect . . . Hamnet said. *I hate buildings.*

You can't hate buildings, she lectured. *You can hate people or guns, but not places, not buildings. They transcend all that. Buildings are blameless. Like water, or air.*

I've always hated buildings.

You're not going to throw in the towel, are you? Not now, not after we've come this far.

Is it any wonder where he gets his acting abilities? Eduardo winked over at me.

What about Houghton, Gertrude went on. *I thought you*

liked this man. He's a great genius and he's your advisor. What more could you want?

To be the man I'm supposed to be . . .

You're not ready.

A man shouldn't obey his destiny? Eduardo wanted to know.

Of course he should, if he should. But why now? she said, touching her husband's arm.

The tide resists the moon at its own peril, not the moon's, Eduardo, trying to express what could not be expressed. He sat forward, frustrated by the inadequacy of his adopted language.

Does everything have to be a metaphor, darling? Let's be objective for a moment. He doesn't have the one thing an . . . "actor" absolutely needs: a wife.

Hamnet stood up then, as though pushed. He didn't know where to look or what to say. It was a force, knotted into a face. For a moment I thought he wasn't going to master himself.

How am I supposed to find a wife . . . when you chase them all . . . to the fucking loony bin? He was shaking from the effort to control himself.

Why are you saying this to me? Gertrude hollered, magnificently injured.

I loved her, he croaked.

How could you . . ?

Picking up bits of debris from the runway, the Concorde lifted off. Above the scrawl of Paris it pinned Hamnet to his seat. The patchwork fell away as they climbed into the turning cavernous dusk. Over the Atlantic the aircraft approached the speed of sound and the setting sun paused and began to rise in the cabin windows. The idea of flying seemed so unnatural. But when choice was removed, Hamnet could surrender it, the obsessive hold he had on himself that only gave way under sacrifice. Imagining death as a similar experience, he was like an unclenching hand.

The eastern seaboard came gradually into view; like a continent on fire, mostly lost in the haze. His awareness of the people around him returned: faces swollen to the size of windows, to the mach metre on the cockpit wall, listening with their eyes. Disturbing technical details crowded into consciousness, the mechanics of landing gear, the gravity of seatbelt buckles; fear and hope rushing to fill a void, their bodies returning to the upright position. Streets appeared below them, a grid of the more personal, like crawling out on a narrow ledge. Then reverse thrusters fastened them tightly to the ground.

The plane stopped short of the terminal and Hamnet was surrounded by gracious flight attendants and a pilot who appeared from the cockpit door to shake his hand. A large number of people were waiting for him, cheering, as stairs appeared beneath his feet. He was overwhelmed on the tarmac by flashbulbs and questions, then a white limousine appeared beside him.

You see, my boy, said the grinning, track-suited Houghton. *Didn't I tell you?*

Hamnet whispered, *I need more time to think.*
I find that time tends to think for itself.
It's too soon.
Look at them and tell me that, Houghton said, referring to the people around the car.
How much did you have to pay them?
Houghton shook his head sadly.
You can't put a price on loyalty, he said. *You're their hope for better looking times.*
Why me?
Ah yes, Houghton said after a thoughtful pause. *Your quest. What was it again? Revenge?*
Justice.

There were plenty of witnesses to the shooting of Hamnet's father, citizens who made indistinct recordings or took blurry pictures. A profusion of viewpoints made it impossible to discriminate the true marksman. Out of the ground of contradictions grew the spectacle, complete with clowns and trained animals and a deaf mute man, who, of all witnesses, Hamnet found most credible.

He was poignant, and, in his own way, dignified. His overcompensating body language and exaggerated facial expressions made a kind of sheepish monster out of him, some lowest common denominator for the TV crews that crowded in behind them waiting for something to happen as the deaf mute man and his wife talked to each other in American Sign.

The fire-eater will speak in halos, the man signed.

The trapeze artist will fall from the sky, she replied.

And the deaf mute man, Hamnet breaks in, signing as well, *mocks the pundits again.*

Their hands stopped moving.

If you can get past the anger, he adds.

You learned to sign, the deaf mute man remarks, stating the obvious.

Hamnet signs, *Is there anything you need?*

The first time Hamnet met this pair, the wife had done his translating and it had been impossible to know which of them he was talking to. The wife was offended that she was no longer needed in the same way and went to the sink to let off steam, throwing some pots into it. When she returned she said they could use some groceries. One of his aides was dispatched.

How have you been? Hamnet asked with his hands, and with his voice for the whir behind him.

Deaf and mute, came the silent reply.

Have you remembered any other details? Hamnet asked him.

He shook his head. What he'd seen that day so long ago was a man running with a rifle, a dark crouch, a shadow merging with a car that sped away. He only agreed to Houghton's request for an interview because he knew Hamnet would give him the benefit of the doubt.

Ask him if he's ever seen a UFO, was heard from outside. Some of the neighbours were peering over their fences.

Let me ask you this, Hamnet signed.

Shoot, the deaf mute man signed back.

How is it possible . . . for a person, any person, to be sure of anything?

I'm sure you're not your father. The man was exhausted, tired, trying hard to prove something, anything.

Hamnet stared at the illusive eyes. He couldn't think of any more questions. Truth didn't take kindly to being prodded. He was thinking he should pack it in, disappear into the Midwest with Ophelia. She wasn't perfect, but at least she accepted him, with all his vanities and his bad acting. He could change his name, join a theatre company.

Ophelia had tossed her medications into the toilet, brave girl, and refused to see more specialists or talk to journalists. Her parents were worn out by their predicament, and were seeking ways to stop making matters worse. They just wanted their normal lives back, but normal was a mythical kingdom someplace in an imagined past.

And reality was drab and ordinary, and Ophelia started going for longer walks and sitting in coffee shops, watching the talkers talk, and marvelling at how well-equipped they were to handle all the time they had on their hands. But she was a tree falling in the forest, a briefly lifted mask, wind chimes foreshadowing storm.

At home she wasn't allowed to watch the rapid eye movement of a sleeping world, but out there TVs were everywhere, like flies. Flickering in restaurants, abandoned on dumpster lids, reflecting on whatever the moment happened to be passing. Grey stone buildings, the same old face, rainy afternoons and buses that didn't stop where a young woman waited for inspiration that didn't come. And then it happened, Hamnet popped up, in the window of the TV store, bodyless from his trans-Atlantic flight, multiplied, grinning in perfect unison with himself. But Ophelia saw his smile was forced, that he was out of his body, that he was overwhelmed, alone.

One evening she was walking past his apartment, trying to remember which balcony it was. There was a man smoking, the shadow of a housecoat watering plants, but no familiar way of leaning. The next day she found a coffee bar across the street. She sat there watching the light, until the shows ended and the critics converged, and the twelve-step groups had reconvened at the tables around her.

She was getting up to leave when she saw him. He was alone, hands abandoned in his pockets. She followed him across the street as far as the gate, where she stopped, snagged on her own reflection. She looked like a nightmare, she had nothing to say. The lobby lights prevented his seeing her there, only a few feet away, as he waited for the elevator. She walked away. It was for the best. But by noon the next day she was sitting at the same nerve-ending, twisting up another napkin.

For Hamnet to light on her finger like a bird, all she needed to show him was that she knew his secret and that she could be trusted with it. But it wasn't that simple, was it? She hadn't counted on there being two of us the next time they met. She came out of her door and there she was. She took a deep breath and words came, not the ones she'd rehearsed, but effective ones nonetheless, sounding clear and sane, and mightily encouraged by Hamnet's reaction. It was the way he smiled, a smile within a smile. But nemesis, like a bit of straw on the wind, his self-doubt, it pierced him, forced him to experience loss as gain, to mistake distance for being there. She saw him slipping away and began to flail, afraid to hit him and afraid to not hit him.

Awkwardly he held her forearms, like the Tin Man, shouting, creating a scene on the sidewalk. When his eyes glazed over like that, Hamnet was gone, imagining himself on some nightmare stage, as some odd character, with the coldest hands in the world.

Your mother was right, I said to him, and it broke the spell. Ophelia pulled free and vanished into the crowd on the other side of the street. Hamnet studied my face, bewildered and hapless, wondering how it would come across if he went after her.

It was about a week later, I don't remember exactly, the morning she climbed out on a ledge and stood there in the cold wind, wearing a sad smile and a summer dress. The dreaming monster had woken up and it crowded on the street below. Hamnet was wrenched from his sleep by his campaign manager and flown to the square in a police helicopter, his mouth still tasting like mouth, his feet in mismatched socks.

Ophelia? Hamnet spoke into the megaphone, his voice metallic and distant.

I loved you, she cried, though the wind tore her words.

If we could rewind the tape . . .

What could you possibly say that I haven't already heard? she shouts.

You wouldn't believe me.

Something authentic and beautiful in his voice. She thought how he was the only one capable of letting her be. Not complete, but whole. He lifted the megaphone again, but because he was Hamnet, he paused. With all his imperfections, could she take it, his bad acting, his wounded name?

Then the building slipped from her hand and she made a terrible silence on the street. Hamnet sat beside her for the last hour, where the hospital had caught her in its web of lines.

It seemed to me funerals were a more authentic affair. They stripped you down to what made you go, down to your basic counterfeits. No maids of horror slumped in a bad sugar crash, no fresh haircuts bleeding soul, like at weddings where hypocrisy played the minister, or the best man, all ill-fitting with rented clothes. But at a funeral, hypocrisy was the leading actor, the guest of honour, the groom, decked out and never before so handsome. Ophelia's parents should have cremated the poor little bitch, left her out with the trash, if they'd wanted to be consistent.

Their family and friends closed around her casket and stood guard over the guest book, forming a barrier between futility and compromise, the sealed remains of everyone's expectations.

Behind police barricades hundreds waited. The spectacle of Ophelia's death had come and embraced Hamnet. One of the magazines had named him the sexiest widower of the year. A receiving line formed wherever he happened to be standing. Acquaintances and writers offered condolences that felt like congratulations.

Ophelia appeared, no more than a few feet away, looking not directly at him. She wasn't interested in any Brueghelesque nightmare, only that Hamnet should see her; and when he did and looked again, she vanished.

Hamnet and Gertrude went for a walk through the rows, between the monuments of notorious friends. They wandered about the prosaic epitaphs of forgotten politicians. Weed-eaters and lawn mowers chewed at the undiscovered silence. They always landed on the same square, between the same parentheses, like a fixed game of chance. They stared at the ground for a few moments, until they couldn't sustain the effort to feel whatever it was they were supposed to feel. Hamnet's hand was aching from an old injury. Gertrude was lost in the grass next to her first husband's grave.

So young, Gertrude said, taking her son's arm, leading him away, *to have your heart broken again.*

What are you talking about?

She was a lovely girl, in her way.

You couldn't stand her.

I could so stand her. It was just . . . I don't know.

Ophelia appeared again and motioned that Hamnet should follow; and Gertrude, unaware, tagged along with a ghost.

It's so short for some, too long for others, she said.
What is?
Precisely, my dear. Winter.
Are you feeling all right?
Of course. Why do you ask? I feel fine.
After a few more steps, Hamnet asked:
Would you like one of these? referring to a stone cross Ophelia was floating over.
No, really, Gertrude said. *It's just this catharsis, I always feel it at funerals. It goes to my head.*

The final act exaggerated the significance of human life. Ophelia's mother was turning everything to mud and her father went on impersonating a cliff. The minister sprinkled water, waved a holly branch. What did it matter? She was just a girl who didn't know Hamnet very well, if at all. She was wrong. And yet she was all he had left. At the wake, Hamnet seemed determined to self-destruct, he got drunk and made provocative statements, showed that he knew shit about shit. He was coming across badly, making everyone nervous. Eduardo appeared at his elbow and steered him to a safer crowd and called for his car. Gertrude held herself up on his arm while they waited at the curb. She was telling him about her plans to live permanently in Spain.

That's when we pulled up in Houghton's limo, cutting in front of Eduardo's car. Hamnet freed his arm from his mother and climbed in. He looked at Houghton who was wearing a bereaved expression and smelled of mothballs and then long and hard at me.

My dear boy, said Houghton, *I'm so—*

I'm not going to lie to them, Hamnet said.

Of course not, Houghton chuckled. *And that's the beauty of it.*

The old doublespeak doesn't work anymore, I offered.

We drove to Houghton's office and took the service stairs to the basement. We entered a room filled with architects' models, balsa wood buildings, cardboard trees, then went down a flight of stairs and into a heavily fortified alternate world, through a maze of hallways, past numbered doors, down more flights of stairs.

Hamnet looked at me rather sadly, said, *Horatio* . . . but that was all.

What . . . ? I shrugged, staring at my old friend in disbelief, remembering all the times he'd betrayed me, had tried to hurt me. But then maybe I was remembering it wrong.

Sacrosanct is no longer a virgin, Houghton said to Hamnet, enjoying the echo in the stairwell. *She was raped by necessity. You are their progeny. Even Fortinbras is powerless. Something bigger is pulling us out, something more than politics, more than ideology.*

But there is no more enemy.

Except for the poor, my boy. Except for the poor.

I can't accept that.

Acceptance can hold you, it holds all of history.
I'll expose you.
It's a role you were born to play.

Hamnet didn't seem to be listening anymore. He was a flickering thumb of cool fire. It took the breath away. The Hamnet curse was everybody's curse.

In a play you know by heart, Houghton went on. *Your words will burst in the sky, turn women into slaves, and all men will be fools. You'll look out at the sea of complacency and understand its flow. And you'll get an urge . . . an urge not to resist any longer, an urge to . . . forgive them.*

Waiting for the Sky

It was a morning the beaches slept in, exhausted from the previous night's mauling. The sea was still playful having lain something at our feet, affectionately soaking my shoes when I went to investigate. A typical feline trick.

It was a woolly corpse, like any dead beast, but not at all foreboding. Just kind of slinking there, the tide sniffed at her handiwork and wanted nothing more to do with it. Later I brought my wagon down and hauled it to the field outside the village.

Later she left a dog, a mongrel of unusual design, a small, indifferent creature. I carted it, too, to the field and put it beside the ewe, which had not yet begun to decompose. There was no scavenger's cold flame nor opportunist's ill fame.

A few other men came to see the mystery for themselves. They didn't want to believe me. It couldn't have been as many weeks as I had said. I fingered my hat and sleeved off some of the sweaty sun. And a fear of the sea was believed to be the cure.

While the other boys were taught about dinghies, I was given a hitch and told to go make my way on the roads. But I have strayed near the water and she has snatched me from the rocks and forced me between her thighs and made me know her.

The next corpse caused more of a stir. Significantly, it was a cat. Everyone wanted to not believe this. The sea was feline herself. A cat approaching a body of water is the soul of prudence, mutual nudge.

The first animal still hadn't started to rot and neither had the mutt and the women began to take an interest. Explanations ranged from magic all the way back to magic, and most conceded that it had something to do with the moon. None would agree to butchering the sheep whose flesh was supple as seawater. They were all like that. Everyone had to see this with their groping. This was not a mystery you could dispose of with explanations.

Where sky meets the ocean, there's a line behind the mist, a crease where it folds back to become the clouds. It formed our minds, just the wonder of it, this fixed horizon whose distance approaching always seemed to lengthen. It was the foundation of my many sleepless nights, when I would sit on the rocky shore and stare and sigh until the relentless drumming of tradition furnished me with my doubts. I was afraid she'd open her eyes and discover only me, and not some eminent diver. I didn't even own a boat.

Downbeach I could hear them, the wives in noon voice, singing to their men at sea. Old wisdom says that on the fourth day lost a boatman can make it to the crease and sail into the clouds to watch over the people and troll for birds. They prepare for the day with songs in praise of letting go, by keeping four days' water on board. Losing shore you quickly disorient they say, and the nine directions play tricks with the waves. Everything in a blink, gone the little hamlet, the past and future, the justifiable, though pointless, outrage at your circumstances. You'd have to go insane just to get some perspective. So long as you don't panic, don't waste your energy looking back.

Let them sing.

When the first human body washed in, the apronned wives puffed up with enfeebled efficiency, furious for not knowing what to do. Should they try reviving the poor woman? Did anyone know her? Perhaps. Though plainly she was translucent as kelp and her tatters were unfamiliar.

She was laid out on a bed of grass beside the animals and, like them, she wasn't decaying in the normal way. Daily visits were made by the respectful and the curious, though some complained that good time was being wasted with all the traipsing back and forth. So they had me cart the body to the common so everyone could keep an eye on her.

The next morning, my estranged one left two more corpses, both women, and the sea would not meet my eye. It was a morning of gelatinous gloom. The strange dead were propped up, the three of them together, which seemed friendlier, and someone put the dead cat at their feet. Every day there was some trinket left behind. Hats appeared and perfume wafted over the square from all the fresh flowers people brought. Some mornings, widows of lost fishermen were found sleeping nearby.

Desperate to see my love again I traded the wagon for a boat and got busy learning the ropes. The men offered advice with shaking heads. A carter has no business out there I was told. It takes a lifetime to learn to command the clouds and to teach the fish to march. You don't have a wife, they lectured. Without a woman to shore a man he couldn't survive a day. They suggested I consider one of the widows.

The men were huddled around a corpse on the shore, because they didn't want the women to see, because it was a large man whose grim power had slipped its grasp. They towed him back out and watched against his return. They too emphatically denied anything was wrong and it wasn't long before the wives knew. The widows wanted to know why he hadn't been put with the others. They wanted to know what the men were trying to hide. They wanted to know if the dead man was one of theirs.

I was learning the boat's inept magic, admiring its wobbly gravity. I went scrabbling near shore, learning the complicated rituals of keeping in sight of land.

Children played around the corpses and the women brought chairs so they could listen for something they couldn't explain. The men stood by and watched, too troubled to risk going out, not sure of themselves, not sure of their wives.

In the morning the men were silhouetted x's against a rising red sun. They hadn't seen one like it in years and it made them optimistic. Several of the wives came down to see it. They agreed it could mean there would be no more surprises.

   I puttered about in the shallows trying to untangle my doubts when a cumbersome wind inflated my sails and by the time I'd talked myself out of it I was quite far out to sea. Then there was a bump against the little craft, followed by another. A pig went floating by, several giraffe. I looked back at the sun-slashed figures on shore. They may have been waving, perhaps they were singing. I couldn't tell. Then they were gone, and the village and the cliffs behind them. And soon I lost sight of land completely. That's when she appeared, climbing some spiral staircase of steam, calming my shivers. She touched my cheek and I set sail for the crease, any direction would do, what water I had was enough.

The Shift

> *Know thyself.*
> —Socrates

> *Wisdom begins when a man realizes he does not know what he thinks he knows.*
> —Plato

> *Goodbye Ruby Tuesday*
> *Who could hang a name on you*
> *When you change with every new day*
> *Still I'm gonna miss you*
> —The Rolling Stones

1. A Bridge

Janitor stands on the roof of the old gym looking through his telescope at the bridge. He studies the jumble of dwellings beneath it, the stacked busses and sideways containers, the spaces between them where maybe another thousand live. Steam rises from openings with the stench of distilled spirits, which from this distance he can't smell, though they blow far enough on memory's breeze. Perspiring a thin layer of rust, the eternal towers adorned with graffiti are draped in rope ladders and fishing nets. An ancient superhero is climbing the web unrehearsed, high above the deck, high above the dried-up harbour, making for the top of the southeast tower. Or is this one supposed to be a bird? A mob will have gathered on the mud flats below, others hanging off the superstructure to watch. It's the only theatre in town. The Greeks and the Elizabethans and the Absurdists all squeezed into one short performance. If it was a good one, somebody might do the honourable thing and dig a shallow grave. Janitor wants to shut it down, plug up the holes, put the stills to better use. Clean water he could trade for 'shrooms, or poor quality speed. Escape is more valuable than gold. More valuable than escape is cancellation, with its headless glimpse of reality, and only ganja can do that. But it takes water to grow weed and that makes it the rarest of the rare.

Janitor was on the roof so early this morning he forgot to put on his watch. He was out at dawn to watch movement on the bridge, working on his strategy, and he was still there hours later when his daughter left the building for her morning rounds with her new guard. Janitor had dismissed her previous escort, Romero, because of his attraction to her, but this new kid was keeping his eyes to himself.

Janitor was in the habit of watching out for her, scanning subtext for a turning page of intuition. He had made of himself a bridge for her to cross to safer times. It was the only thing he could do. He brought her into this world, cut from the cooling mother, delivered into his shaking hands, giving him the strength to live, to slit a thousand throats, the resolve to survive a thousand deaths.

Her guards aren't old enough to hold memories of Before Times. If you were born after the disintegration, you knew nothing. This guard is quick and clever but his heart is still a cherry, his naiveté troubling. He has a soldier's level gaze, but does he know any more than his place in a world where remorseless killing is still your best asset? Janitor doubts it. A throbbing pain in his mouth swamps his thoughts, one rotten tooth after another. He works on one with the hilt of his long knife, wishing it out, pushing.

He named her Butterfly, because she was like a first flower in the wasteland. She has his knack for assuming nothing, a love of bad situations, the best qualities of a good general.

Most of them fear too much and believe too little, that's about all that hasn't changed. Superstition suits their spells for cleaning murky water, incantations of self-regard, a sentimental snobbery. It is a language spoken in shards, a string of pearls without a thread, a book on standing translated from the dominos.

He climbs off the roof and goes in a side door, down to the basement where the water purification plant is operating. They didn't have the tools, or the right equipment, or enough expertise, but somehow they managed. Using his science background, Tom McBeth was able to see it all come together. Between them they got all this scrap working—the boilers and the pipes stoked with a constant dirty fire to distil enough water for their needs and to do a little trading with the neighbourhoods.

Janitor goes down the hall past the former classrooms where they've made laboratories, sick bays, rooms for the dogs, rooms full of homemade spears and swords, lockers full of slings and worthless firearms now used as clubs. He thinks ammunition is being controlled from somewhere, by something, some ad hoc authority, a remnant branch seizing control of cobwebs. The soldiers kept coming until they stopped coming. It was government of the people by the people for the people. More bullets would come in handy.

In the cafeteria, Tom is at his usual place in front of the chessboard. Something about his expression disorients, giving Janitor the feeling of being sapped, in the dark about something. Probably just his tooth.

What time is it? Janitor asks when he sits down.

After you've removed the other eleven?

Don't . . .

A ragged old soldier sitting nearby looks at his gold watch and grins, *You're early this morning, General.*

Tom sets up the chessmen between them and without a word they start a game, Tom leading with a pawn two spaces. The General, Janitor, looks at the board and makes a thoughtless move, waiting for the voice, as though he was initiating with the white instead of responding with the black, making each move a crisis in confidence. Janitor is looking at the fly on the white queen. Aiming for the air six inches above the board, he snatches for the fly. He expected to scare it into his closing hand as proof of his legerdemain. But he's off this morning and sends the chessmen flying.

The soldier's willingness to follow Janitor depended on his reflexes, and when these were breached, even slightly, they felt the abyss crack open just a little.

I was trying to catch the fly, he says, reassuringly re-establishing a state of least resistance, which they huddle around like a flame.

A fly? Tom makes it sound like he doesn't believe him.

You saw it there . . .

There are many kinds of flies.

An ordinary housefly.

Ask yourself this, Tom says after he's got the game set up again. *When a fly has approximately ten thousand eyes, why does he find wallpaper so interesting?*

This time Janitor is white and he takes back his first move, just so he can move a different pawn. After law and order collapsed, the army confiscated people's firearms. The ones who hadn't registered them became local powers. Whoever killed the most lived longest; it was natural selection on speed. In the aftermath, sex was the only drug. It wasn't the self-esteem you sought but the narcotic of seeking.

How long will it take to convert the stills, integrate them into the system?

Depends on when we take the bridge?

Tom stares at his friend, for so long the only thing standing between him and the barbarians. When this nightmare began, all the teachers could do was stand there. None of them knew what to do.

I think Butterfly was out an hour early this morning. Did she say anything to you?

How's your toothache?

A peaceful sadness envelops him. This was treasure, humanity's walking with fire. From significance you de-concluded, understanding was impossible. Amidst collapse you saw it, a vertical shimmering against the buckling horizontal.

Romero . . . Janitor says, realizing, the clouds parting. Like a smell in the air, the feeling when everybody else knows something. Something they think you don't want to hear. Romero, her last guard, that's why she snuck out, that's where she was now.

Romero has potential, Tom feels compelled to say.

Is it enough?

Don't be a fool...

Janitor stares at his friend. Just then Butterfly comes into the room. Most of the men turned to look at her, but with the General sitting right there it chafed, and they went back to their private thoughts.

I've been looking for you, she says to her father. *Why aren't you at home? Do you know the time?*

Where is your guard? he asks her.

Standing outside.

He taught her to ignore self-doubt, distinguish between intuition and its counterfeits. He knew the time had come for his last push. That there be a shore for her to reach, that was all he asked.

This Romero is unproven...

No...

So, who isn't? Tom interjects.

You're in on this? What is this, a plot? Janitor stands up, impotently threatening.

On the ledge of tears, Butterfly thinks she knows something, that Janitor was seeing something she couldn't see. But she was years ahead of him in knowing what she will do. She is in a different universe already, with Romero.

He's waiting for me, she says out loud, something meant as a private thought.

Call him in.

When Romero is standing in front of him, Janitor motions his daughter to the side and proceeds to poke the young man's chest with his finger, to see what he's made of, ready to be convinced one way or the other.

Where is your honour?

Here is my knife. Romero pats his thigh.

The General pushes and the young man falls to the floor.

Father . . .

This is unnecessary, announces Tom.

I swear, Janitor says, laughing, *that if he does not at this moment make the correct noises . . .*

Romero stands, weighing his knife, holding it in one hand, then the other. What the General has lain at his feet is bigger than he knows. The old man's display was badly aimed, but effective. Romero had one choice, no in-betweens, no returns. Were Butterfly's best chances with her father or him? Gravity is working on Romero's dagger, waiting for the carry-through impulse he knows must come. But he's disturbed because the General's intention is unclear, ill-advised.

Unmasked . . . Janitor grins.

Romero downcast, mutters, *Useless old tit.*

He casts a helpless glance at Butterfly. His losses quickly multiplying, he crashes out the main door. There is a moment of humiliation and Butterfly is stuck there, then she flies out the other door, through the kitchen, and into the school proper. Janitor feels something slip out of his grasp. McBeth slides out, following the girl.

A moment later the alarm sounds. A band of killers, fuelled by hooch and impatience, strike at the school's perimeter guards. It's too fast to respond. The men are falling, there is confusion in every act. The attackers begin to overwhelm the school. Janitor's blows fall short, the blade of his long sword hits wide.

Then Romero and two lines of fighters flush the attackers into a trap, the General squeezing in with his men to cut them off. They kill them all except for one, a crazed animal who slips past them and gets into the school.

Who has Butterfly? asks Romero.

I . . . Janitor realizes his failure. With all his preparations he wasn't there.

He and Romero start searching, their friends fanning out behind them, calling through every space.

Outside the gym, their torches blazing, they hear a wet cry from within. They run and catch the animal in the final act of rape. Naked blood jumps like quicksilver. Janitor yells to drown out the sound of tearing flesh as he charges across the room. Much too late in skewering the killer, his dainty breaths so like a child's it sickens him. Romero kneels beside her, dust from her wings on his fingers.

Romero staggers to his feet and runs at the General, breaking his blade on the bone of his breastplate, then runs away into the gloom. The General stands there, swimming in his own rank mouth, shaking.

Tom is there in the shadows, the sagging floor marshalling all the blood to the centre.

Other neighbourhoods are attacking now, Tom says.

Good, Janitor says, meaning a different world, tragedy's unspeakable gift. Good, what a brief face, what a small banishment from the alien duststorms of the shift.

Tom pulls him away, and through a seldom-used side door, takes him out of the old stone building where they move cautiously under the sky's trivia. Tom leads them towards the bridge, because beyond it lies the mountains, forest, where he imagined himself growing up. It was now just a matter of crossing.

For a quarter of a mile on the causeway through the forest, they see no one. But as they approach the carved lions guarding the bridge's southern proscenium, a handful of men appear and block their way.

Why aren't you men out fighting your war? Janitor rumbles at them.

We expected a slightly larger force, General.

But she's gone, don't you understand? Janitor shouts at them. *I have no reason to attack you any more.*

What a strange man you are, one of them says.

Admit it General, says another.

I'm this nobleman's servant, Janitor points at Tom. *I'm just here to help my good sir cross the bridge. I tell him jokes. But he doesn't laugh . . . I dance . . .*

Why's he need to cross the bridge? asks the mouthiest one. *Why doesn't he just go around? The harbour is dry. There's no water in the bay. In case you haven't noticed, there's no Georgia Strait. So why don't you just quit bullshitting us?*

He brought us this lunatic, so let's see him dance, says their leader.

Janitor is standing there, caught in the beginning of a strange and beautiful dance. Tom climbs past the barricade of smashed cars and disappears in the maze of haphazard sheeting. When Janitor realizes his friend is gone he whirls on his attackers and they ride him down.

Tom makes it past the distracted habitations, gets through their grimy reflections and complacent stench. Getting closer to the other side, he's already thinking about the perpendicular wilds and going under nameless mountains.

2. The Collectors

Field put up his hand to halt the group. Only his marshals obeyed: his two emaciated assistants carrying the ladder. He ordered them to set it up and hold it steady, an old cherry-picker like one from the farm when he was a kid. He went up the twenty steps to a little platform on top. From this vantage point above the viscous haze he could survey their position relative to his expectations. He took a bearing from the crag in the distance, some pile of cliffs. Their faces changed: unfamiliar, contradictory, always throwing him. He fingered the St. Christopher around his neck and tried to discriminate landmark from shadow. The sun was wrong, not coming, not going, but pulling along the horizon like a snail on a foot of bending light.

The exposed mantle shape-shifted into a different thing every time he looked. His deputies stared up at him with a wry kind of blankness, waiting for some inane comment that they wouldn't feel obliged to respond to. He sneered at them. He wouldn't mind getting some encouragement, some kind of response; but whatever he'd do what needed to be done.

He rotated his arms out for balance like he was waltzing with himself, turning to face the other way, the night, the wall of darkness that sat there. It didn't come anymore like a nursemaid, or an undertaker, dependably to cover you with its blanket, to tuck you in. It sat there and you had to go to it, bearing the world on your back. The moon was gone, but the earth survived. Field didn't much go in for speculation. Maybe it was a comet or something. He didn't see it happen. All he knew, like everyone else, is that it wasn't there anymore. The rotation of the planet was altered too, which added to the difficulty. It had slammed into the Canadian Shield, whatever it was. Like the white dot on an eight ball, or an old 45 RPM wobbling without an adaptor, the impact crater permanently facing the sun.

Two hundred and counting lost souls, carrying the dismantled collectors, pushing against their limitations. Subsumed in the emotion of thirst, they passed slowly beneath him in the soupy haze.

Jocko was the strongest amongst them and he hadn't returned as per his usual pattern. He went off for days and returned with enough extra water for his daughter. Nobody knew where he went for it, and he wasn't much of a talker. Maybe the move threw him off. Maybe the desert finally got him.

Jocko's daughter walked under the ladder and grinned up at him and he quickly looked away. Getting lost was his biggest fear. Young women and objectivity did not mix. What good was love if it was only good for making life infinitely more complicated? Man, the paragon of animals. At sixteen she had the physiognomy of a killer. Prematurely aged. Did it make her that much sweeter? He didn't want to know.

Her smile mocked him, mocked his seriousness. He hated it when people did that. Could she not see what lay ahead? Was she heartless as well as jailbait? It amazed him that even here, even now, man was not free of this old curse.

And where the fuck was Jocko? Maybe the desert did get him. But it was too soon to start indulging in superstitions, vain hopes, petty wishes. Nothing possessed you like dehydration. It forced you to tear open the dead. You'd trade what you had for a jar of piss or go for a swim in the sand, do the butterfly, and learn the crawl. And there was one price, one price for everything: water.

The shifting hues of the wasted landscape looked beautiful in the eternal sunset. Field took another bead on the puzzling distance. The Great Lakes had been blasted into space, leaving the exposed mantle to bake. Vapour from the frozen oceans was sucked into the overheated basin and great falls of mist rose into the sky in unbelievable amber-yellows, and was pissed away into the atmosphere.

His lads hiked the ladder onto their shoulders and started after the group. It was a risky decision to move, maybe his last one. They were moving the collectors in search of better air, wetter air, going further into the terminator's deeper setting. If they weren't careful they might never find their way back out.

Conditions varied depending on how you wanted to set up, or how deep into the atmosphere you were able to reach, though differences from place to place were negligible and hard to quantify. The output at the collectors' previous location was low. Though they hadn't started losing so many people until now.

Gradually, as the ether got duskier and their elevation gradually increased, they could taste a difference in the air. Their breath came easier, spirits fluttered. When he discovered moisture forming on his beard, Field gave the order to set up camp.

Comparable individuals collapsed for a few hours' sleep in their dream-like shelters made of sticks and pieces of clothing. A curious thing. How real could the world be, if it vanished so simply, so completely in sleep?

Trouble was, it didn't stay vanished. The process of re-erecting the collectors got under way. Without Jocko helping, their progress was slow. It was a technical job that was more art than science.

When the masts were up, they had two smaller ones that stood five storeys high and the main one that reached between them was nearer to ten. When the masts were anchored and braced, the collector panels went up one at a time, like sails woven from the guts of Before Times, from harp strings to the finest spider-goat silk: the mangled filaments of progress, woven into a membrane so fine it captured the molecules right out of the air, collapsed it down to water.

From his perch, Field fine-tuned the rigging, tightened the weave. He balanced the feed lines that led to the main arteries that would carry the drops, one at a time, painstakingly assembling them in a pail below. Or not, depending how successful he was at recognizing the moment when he needed to leave well enough alone. There was no manual, no plan. Rehearsals in his mind just made reversals in the air. Something had to be moving in two directions at once, as in the conservation of energy, before the beads of water actually started to form.

It was a simple thing, this dying slowly. Why they even bothered with all the survival shit was beyond him. For some reason you had to *keep on truckin'*, leftover ethics of circadian times. How could you feel anything but misery and longing? Sometimes when the sun caught the collectors just so, they shone with a melancholic kind of majesty, bathed in an undreamt-of passion. Sometimes he could almost feel it, a sense of mystery, a blade turning, a kind of holding on that was, in truth, letting go.

Two deaths occurred during the wait for water. The bodies were dragged out of sight and Field said a few words over them, from some fragment he remembered:

So much depends upon . . . the white chickens beside . . . the red wheelbarrow.

When they had enough water for everyone, Field had some and crawled under one of the wagons and tried to sleep. He kept a bottle nearby to recycle his urine in. He shut his eyes and a drum started beating. Jocko was back. His daughter would be dancing. The men with their burdens of doom would be around her, looking mean, slipped one notch up from despair. Their madness would lift slightly to reveal their hunger.

He gave up and went over to watch. The girl's body calmed him, looking at it, how the space she occupied was tighter, a steady expansion and contraction of her spine. That's when it hit him, the realization that he would kill for her, with his bare hands if necessary. One of the men was waving his shirt at her as she danced around him. Lurching to grab the girl, he fell on her shadow. Smith, always the fool. The thought of what Field needed to do calmed him and he went to sleep for a while imagining ways of killing Jocko. Problems were simpler in the higher dimension of dreaming. Where two and two equalled five, where things locked and unlocked at the same time.

A lizard scrabbled over the sand by his face and Field awoke and grabbed it, broke its back, and put it in his pocket. He was thinking about Jocko. If Jocko went for his knife, would he be able to stop him? And then what? He needed to be sure.

Longing for things of the past drew people together like fireflies to their own accumulated light. It was all they had, this dump of wanting, this closeness none had sought, which few had experience in. To be identified with fitting in, because they had no clocks, natural or mechanical, to tell them how they shouldn't feel.

The rituals they carried, like trinkety possessions that hadn't been discarded yet. Jocko's drumming, his daughter's dancing, Field's silly good-luck charm, a gift his brother gave him to keep him safe in his travels.

Field couldn't keep his mind on his task. What was it? His objective, his duty, his priority slipped to the side. Field tried to settle his mind but there was Jocko's back. That was it. Several quick thrusts with his knife. But was that really it?

When Jocko left camp again, his long shadow was planting footprints in the wind. Was the extra distance wearing him down? Field watched him from the top of the main mast, his subconscious mind still working away on murder. Then another shadow emerged from the outcroppings of rock, another elongated silhouette. Smith's, following the madman into the desert.

Smith soon seemed to come to the end of his road. As Field watched, he tottered for a moment, looking around from where he'd come. And then, as though accepting his fate, he fell. *Stupid bastard; won't last long.*

But what was this? Jocko returned, picking up the weather-beaten Smith, hoisting the man on his shoulder like a rolled rug and proceeding on his initial track.

How long would he be gone this time? Ten or twelve rotations of the sun? Field didn't know. Without Jocko they were short-handed. Without Jocko, Field could approach the girl without fear.

When's he coming back? he asked her, his shadow courteously lying over her face.

Her eyes narrowed in a little smile.

He's miles away by now, he said. And to reassure himself as to that point he looked around, seeing no threatening silhouette, no awkward shoulders. He knelt beside her, took the dead lizard from his pocket and gave it to her.

She kissed him. Her lips were curious. He enjoyed it; it was innocent. She fingered the medal dangling at his neck.

What's wrong? she asked.

Is something wrong?

Why won't you give me this?

You wouldn't understand.

It's too important to you. That makes it a curse. You should give it to me to break the curse.

How's that going to break the curse? Look around . . .

Why can't I just say no to myself when I meet you?

As their bodies merged, her calloused fingers touched him gently and introduced him to her moistness. He gasped, remembering surprise, everything turning for a moment into light, even the shadows, even the rocks.

Emptiness broken open, unexpected charm. What was water in comparison? Nothing more than flattered steam, obsequious ice. And what of the Great Lakes, where were they now? He went to sleep in her arms dreaming of summer rain.

He awoke violently, bouncing on Jocko's back, agony and numbness all jumbled up.

The girl was running beside them, crying, *Don't harm this one, Daddy.*

Jocko stopped running, incredulous. *You haven't fallen for him?*

I don't know. He's different.

She's telling you the truth, man, listen to her, Field hissed, furious with himself for not killing this animal when he had the chance.

Jocko dropped Field painfully to the ground, shrugged and kept on going. His daughter gasped in disbelief, looked down at Field who hadn't gotten up yet, and ran after Jocko. Field couldn't believe her, such a lack of imagination. A bit of romance would have been such a fitting end for the squalid little story of man.

The collectors were far away; without water he'd never make it back. Soon the scavengers would be coming to make of him a last miserable meal. He got to his feet and followed them.

He was coming apart, evaporating one brain cell at a time. As long as he accepted the inevitable, his mind remained reasonably sharp. When he started remembering the way it was, he became disoriented, thinking back on the days when everything ran on fumes. He kept obsessing about those little dogs with springy heads you used to see in people's cars.

He found steam rising from a crack in the rocks and found a small pool of odd-smelling water. He dipped his hand to sniff at it, drank a few handfuls and sat back on his haunches to wait for the likely poisons to take effect. A hot breeze batted at him.

He saw a narrow passage through the rocks and followed their tracks into a cave, which turned into a honeycomb of disorientation. But it didn't matter where he died, only that he died with dignity. He didn't know why that was. It sounded absurd. He passed out and had a dream that he was having a dream about dreaming.

He awoke and found himself back between Jocko's shoulder blades. It disgusted him, the muscles moving in and out, the bones sawing away to the rhythm of being chewed.

Down they went, his little angel holding a hand, his hand that had lost all feeling, down through the diaphanous darkness. Feeling their way along the edges, through passages of pain, knocks that forced them to crawl.

They stopped for a mouthful of water. Contrition, humility, friendship, lust, vexation, rancour, fear, and more blackness. When Jocko turned and punched him in the face it was a relief to feel something so personal and unambiguous.

He went willingly now. A little stronger yet. Agonies created out-of-body experiences.

Then there was a light. A forty-watt bulb. It was hanging in the viscous air. Around them in the dimness were broken parts of buildings, torn rooms. An old man, monk-like in appearance, separated himself from the rock, and Jocko dropped to his knees. Was he exhausted, finally?

The old man took the girl's face in his hands and his expression changed, trying to pin something down. He approached Field and examined his hands, his face, his teeth. Bringing his fist up he tested his reflexes. Chuckled to himself.

Where's the power come from?

The old man considered Field's question but didn't answer.

Following a rope attached to the wall of the cave, they moved swiftly. The air was cooler now, and there were occasional dimly lit areas over difficult terrain, places where you rested a moment before going on. Field felt good to be on his feet, to be moving.

A sound was growing as they travelled toward its source. More dim bulbs revealed sections of massive pipe, sometimes hidden by rock, a din sometimes exposed, and leaking water. It was the intake of a hydro plant, a raging river in a can. He put his hand on the cold steel and felt the vibration of its bones.

Finally they came out under a moonless sky. Stars provided what light there was. It brought tears to his eyes; at least there was still this, the Milky Way. And an aurora fluttering like a curtain at an open window.

Suddenly, blindingly, stadium lights came on, exposing, in that moment, the grubs: women with expressionless faces and men with bad backs. They were worm farmers. They were technicians. There were crashed bleachers, stages, hundreds of tombstones piled into great stacks . . . no, speaker cabinets. Then it was dark again.

Music came on. Wagnerian, criminally loud, a slow mournful pummelling under the stars. Field asked if anybody knew where Jocko's daughter was, but no one could possibly have heard him.

After the operatic bludgeoning the lights came on again and Field stood up to look for the girl. Then Stravinsky started thrashing his senses about, as he tried to stand up and walk. The lights went out before his eyes could adjust, and then he saw nothing.

He wept himself into a state of dehydration, accompanied by

the familiar symptoms of misery. Then somebody was giving him water, sweet and fragrant. Images lingered like ghostly snapshots after they tested the lights. One time he thought he saw her, and it looked like she was looking for him.

It registered on Field that somebody nearby was crying. He wanted to say something, but something in the sound of it terrified him. He didn't want to know what it was that made this poor fucker unclench his heart in such perfect sorrow. As the hours unfolded into the endless steady night it finally got to Field, the steady trickle of regret, and he said, *Stop . . .*

There was silence, then a familiar, *Field? That you?*

Smith?

You poor sorry son of a bitch . . .

A dim light went on over Smith, attendants were washing him. They shaved his body and stood him up in a loincloth. They chained his neck and without further ado led him out. Field's cage looked out on a stage where they were leading Smith out under the lights, accompanied by an audience of hundreds, all moaning and shouting and laughing.

In the centre of the theatre was a big stone ball raised up on a dais, which spun slowly. They strapped Smith to a steel contraption on the ball. What strange orb . . . this moon. That was it. And Smith the comet that shattered it. Men, heads of clans, came filing onto the stage with small knives, forming a circle around this altar.

Jocko was off to the side staring intently at the preparations. His daughter stood beside him, looking at Field.

An old man dressed in white stepped out under the lights and raised his hands. The crowd fell silent. You could hear Smith's whimpering and the squeaking of the apparatus that held him up and turned him around.

The girl's lips were moving in a vainglorious attempt to communicate something to Field. Jocko was watching her, and followed her line of sight past the spectacle to the cage at the back and the faint shadow slumped there.

The signal was given and the impotent had an orgy. One man cut out Smith's tongue while screaming gibberish. Another took off his balls and danced triumphantly away. They stripped away his skin, cut out most of his organs. They were like children at a piñata, one son of a bitch biting off his ears and another tearing away the scalp. Like a horse in the wrong river, Smith was carved down to his skeleton while his heart still beat, suspended in its bloody cage. And one good eye knew well enough what was happening to it. As the crowd roared, Smith couldn't lose consciousness, or even utter any curse.

Field hollowly sobbed. Escaped into the past. The better you held it together the harder it crumbled; like dried insect wings, the structures of memory go. Like scrap in a scrap yard. What was this great missing anyway? What mistake was so monstrous? The vagueness sucked everything in, covered it with a deep imitation. Now they were coming for him, travelling down a different hallway, towards a blacker light, on strange insect legs.

They bathed him and shaved him. They put the chain around his neck. Field heard more footsteps and looked up to see Jocko and his daughter standing in front of him. Jocko took one of the attendants aside and before Field could speak they were removing his chains. Jocko was asking him if he was able to stand— *Yes, he was able to stand*—and to walk, *Yes!*

Then the attendants went to work on Jocko and let Field go. The crowd went wild when they saw Jocko being led out. They chanted his name, rattled and shrill.

Field couldn't understand any of it. Especially the feeling of regret as the girl led him out of the starry hall and down into the tunnels.

He awoke on the ground, the sun pushing at him to get up. Field stood there blinking. He must have fallen. Jocko's daughter had stopped banging her drum, and sat looking at him. He nodded to encourage her to continue, though he couldn't remember what. Some ragged dickhead took over on the drum and allowed her to begin slowly spinning out her dance. Field climbed back up the mast. There were other collectors out there. Shaky little images that depended on how calmly he held his binoculars, on how still he kept his breathing.

3. The Way Station

Space-age blankets formed a serviceable kind of portable shade. They wobbled above him, attached to a shoulder harness constructed of aluminium lawn furniture. Slung from his belt was his last water bottle, empty. He came to a high point and surveyed the desert running before him in every direction. To call it empty was to say too much. Yet it was devoid of anything so . . . . There was a pointless belligerence. There was nothing to get hold of, nowhere to offend the eye, only heat waves distorting what was already changed beyond all recognition.

Something was there, perhaps three miles away, moving steadily, like one of those drinking birds you used to see, up and down, either empty or full, no half measures, impossible and completely reliable. Up. Down. Up. Then nothing. Could it be the station he'd been trying to reach? Sweeny's station was not a myth. It was the last water hole before the last march, before the mountains could be seen.

McBeth put his next foot down. It was all he could do. It was all anybody could do. Anything else was just a product of the mind, what little of it there was left. The flies of regret had lain their eggs. He wasn't going to last much longer. He'd gone further than he expected. He should be dead already. But calculations were for beginners. You either had water or you didn't.

It was strange the way the sun stayed fixed in the sky. When he got to the blessed foothills it wouldn't be so directly overhead. McBeth didn't understand how this was even possible. He was bound to find some kind of shade. Those who attempted the journey before, they all made it to beautiful imagined landscapes. In McBeth's mind, he wandered in circles, duped by his own geography, like a ridiculous ant on a sidewalk. He was attended by shadows that glided over the sand like manta rays, vultures that couldn't believe their luck.

The thing in the distance was moving again. Could it be the rip-tide of a mirage, or the Great Narrator shifting back and forth through versions? No, this was mechanical. But Tom McBeth wasn't going to make it. He jettisoned the empty bottle, but it was too little too late. Tangled up in his shade contraption, he collapsed.

The buzzards landed. Operating as a team, Lucky moved in while Patient practiced their species' instinct for crowd control, even though there were only the two of them—and the man, lying there motionless, partially hidden by a crumpled blanket. Was it the way he fell, perhaps a bit overplayed, that gave them pause? They were cautious, slow-going, as the man watched their crooked teamwork. The larger one wore an imprecatory expression as he took the initiative, reluctantly provocative, probing. McBeth wondered how they could put up with each other, being so ugly?

When the head probed a little too close the man's fingers closed around its throat. Dirty fingers, dirty man. The bird was outraged when it realized its error, the kind it always made. Confidence was not his friend. The claws tagged him a few times and McBeth was surprised he could still bleed. He summoned his last effort and rolled over the bird with enough momentum to snap something. He could feel the scavenger's fury surcease. The remaining bird hopped to a more respectful distance, the last of his kind, companion to the unknown.

McBeth's knife tore the hot carcass before the heart could stop fluttering. He yanked it clear of its trappings and swallowed it like an oyster. He tore up the rest of the bird and ate what he could stomach and left the rest for its friend.

Swimming in and out of consciousness, he strapped on the shade and resumed his journey. The last buzzard spent some time with the carcass and then caught up later. It circled a few times then flew on to investigate what lay ahead.

He was much closer now. The derrick towered over the rest of the station: the flywheel pump, the solar panels, the nests of batteries. There was a man about halfway up hammering something with a spanner and cursing loudly. Tom was ambivalent about hearing the voice of another human, revealing, as it seemed to, vague shapes of things to come. The bird found some shade next to the station. Preening was pointless.

It was Sweeny, had to be. He was covered in thick drying mud. He dropped to the ground between the control panels and threw a switch to the pump. With convulsions, the flywheel got the ground shuddering. Then water gushed from the wellhead, raining down and probing with fingers to the level of new mud.

A woman came out of the station. She ran over and slid into the mud, wallowed in her skimpy dress while Sweeny swung on a valve to redirect the flow down a pipe into a holding tank. The woman had scrawny legs, big useful hands, and extraordinary eyes when she saw Tom McBeth standing there.

Sweeny! her voice was clear.

I saw him, Sweeny said, without looking.

Something to eat? she asked.

Water . . .

She guided him to the door of the station, and inside the air was cool and rank. The room was set up like a bar: a few tables with chairs, the walls covered in oddball shit, shelves of useless stuff. She put a cup of water on a table, pulled out a chair for him. She sat down too and watched him take a tablet from a pouch on his belt.

Smart, she said.

He didn't have many left. He looked at the water, looked at the girl, looked at the purification tablet, then broke it and dropped in half. The other half went back in the pouch. The girl gave him some dried meat and as he chewed he wondered what she was going to say when he told her he couldn't pay for it.

He wound his watch and set the timer.

The place is like a junk store, he commented.

Strange, the things people collect.

His watch gave off the sound of small bells and he picked up the cup, gently swirled it, and drank. The girl disappeared and he moved to the floor. Leaning against the wall, he slipped into sleep. Dreaming about pearls, a string of them, ploughing through space towards nothing.

When McBeth opened his eyes there were other men. Oil lamps were burning. Sweeny sat in a corner studying them. It was unnerving. The girl was probably beautiful, but, like everything else in the station, she was tainted.

A newcomer leaned over. *You headed for the mountains?*

He remembered fish, how movement was the constant, like change, only narrower, to where nothing changed but the odds, which got progressively worse all the time.

Sweeny went out to tend his pumps and the other travellers followed, eager.

You travellers, the girl amused herself, not bothering to finish.

What?

Are you married?

How could that possibly matter? Field was truly surprised.

You and your mountains, you just keep coming.

Are you married to him? he asked.

He is a monster.

He's pretty ugly. What would he do if he saw where your hand is?

What could he do?

I can think of a few unpleasant scenarios.

What can be more unpleasant than this? she asked, looking around her.

I'm not a big fan of pain.

Too bad.

He felt himself becoming aroused. His native reserve winked out, and his fear of consequences disappeared as though behind the turn of a leaf. She straddled him and he vanished under her shift. She started slapping his face, harder, harder, until he unlocked and disintegrated.

She put a handful of dirt in his hand and told him to get rid of the smell. She pushed her hair off her face and went into the other room. Funny, he was thinking, how she thought she saw through him. When he woke again, she was leaning over him with a steaming bowl.

She handed him a fork. He tasted it. Liked it.

What is it?

Your bird.

Oh . . .

Sweeny was ready to start the big engine, so the girl went out for the rain with the other men. Tom hung back, curious about the other room. It was down some stairs, a basement carved out of ash. Something about it, the smell, the terribleness of it. A flash of metal caught his eye. Tacked to a wall, along with a cluster of other jewellery, he found a Saint Christopher's medal. He picked it up and let the cool silver chain drop into his palm like water. He climbed the stairs and ran out into the mud to hide the awful tunnel in his tears.

The other travellers left with water bottles hanging from their belts and tied to either end of ropes that cut into their shoulders. Tom watched to see which direction they followed, if they went with their gut or their head. It was supposedly a few more days' march before the mountains would come into view.

He was thinking hard, trying to decide which way to go, trying to get up his nerve. The only hope was to act, and to act swiftly, without hope. He didn't have time for this. The only thing he ever learned was that nothing from the past prepared you for the present. He had taken a utility knife from the girl, and came up behind Sweeny in the yard.

Sweeny turned around, holding a length of pipe. He saw Tom had a weapon and smiled. Extending the blade on the knife, Tom backed away. When he felt the derrick behind him, he climbed. Sweeny swung mildly at him as they climbed over cables and through rigging. Tom reached the top, the rust-grimy structure no longer grasped in his hands, and held out the knife. Sweeny easily batted it away with his pipe. Then he mocked his prey by doing a little dance on the rickety platform. From below the engine groaned and the flywheel banged and shook the frame, surprising Sweeny. Knocked off balance, he fell from the derrick to the hard-pack earth below.

Tom helped her drag the body into the kitchen and down the stairs. Then he went outside and stood in the small shade off the porch. He wiped sweat from his forehead. He couldn't escape the sound of chopping and his body convulsed painfully around his empty stomach. He sobbed, but stopped when he saw a figure emerging from the heat waves, still several miles away.

Biggs and Little

After six hours non-stop from the coast the two men appear tentative, stiff, on the unnaturally bright sidewalk. Wiry Biggs is bleak with hunger and leading the way. Taller broader and falling behind Little is just glad to be out of the car. When he catches up, his friend is ordering the hamburgers he's been raving about for the past three hours, confessing to the stranger in the window some vague wrong he suspects of himself. Biggs likes to make it a public hanging, the frame-up of his mind. He's an intimate of outsiders but reticent with his only friend, meting himself out in incomplete snatches, gauging and recalibrating his responses according to a shifting standard only he understands. Though he'll relax from grim to gloomy if the inevitable stupidity of the world confirms his worst fears, doom being his only consolation. On a park bench they eat in isolation until their stomachs are full and they have relaxed and stretched their legs out in front of them. Then the fact of their companionship elbows back in. Beyond their dusty shoes, below in the valley, the mighty Fraser runs, self-absorbed and twisted like a hunchback's spine.

Biggs says, *That's one volume of water.*

Little looks at his friend for his body language, to make the words read, though nothing much shows. Does he mean *impressive*, or something unfinished? Often he intends the opposite of what he says or something completely unrelated. He could be commenting on the infallibility of existence or maybe predicting the death of water. Both their pasts are littered with his reversals.

They make for cheap air conditioning, out back of which the CN tracks waver in the heat, a service road's width off their second floor balcony. And beyond, the loping pockmarked river.

I hope a train goes by, Little says.

Biggs doesn't respond, but he brings chairs out and lights a cigarette. His hard eyes rub against the arid valley, the mountain shaped like a woman on her back, the river-parted cliffs in sunset orange. Little's comment elicited no reply but has set in motion Biggs' mental contraption, the steel ball of his attention, through its maze and spirals, its verdicts and flea circus tragedies.

You think I could hit the water with a king cob from here? Or would it take a steely? Biggs asks, distantly, scratching at something by way of the past. As boys they made slingshots every summer, Biggs always improving on the basic design, experimenting with projectiles, greater power. One eye still bothers him.

It's too far, Little says.

Disloyal bastard, Biggs mocks, or seems to.

Apprehension unfolds in Little's stomach like a road map. A familiar feeling, and he hates it.

Biggs says, *Please explain it to me.*

Explain what . . . my friend?

You keep insisting you're my friend, Biggs says, seizing on something, prying at an opening.

Little says, *I am . . .*

What kind of friend never offers to help? Biggs asks, and seeing only bafflement from the other, elaborates, *Me, to realize my true potential.*

You have a lot of potential.

That's the problem.

Little is stumped.

That it's never been allowed to blossom, Biggs allows.

I would have thought you blossomed.

It's like trying to understand a four-way stop on acid . . . Biggs says, meaning Little's logic, dismissing it. He goes inside and lies on the bed away from the sliding door.

If Little stays out of his way until morning maybe things will be back to normal. But then again, this is normal. He decides to go out for Chinese and a six-pack.

Biggs is more sociable after a few and the chemical fragrance rising from the food containers reassures them both. Little thinks about the next day, whether Biggs will be morose and inspire nothing but resistance from potential customers, or be in fighting trim, Mr. Friendly himself, in and out of stores and offices, depending on how cocky he feels, on how many orders they've taken for letterhead, pens and embossed business cards, on how many they've sold of the retractable multi-tools and key chain folding scissors.

A westbound freight labours through the town. Coming straight on, the boxcars wobble an obese conga line behind the engine. Little closes his eyes and leans over the railing, listening to the train's intricate music, its remarkably light touch. Biggs nails a boxcar with a greenie and this pleases him. He counts a hundred and twenty cars, certainly no world record, and without so much as a caboose. The train's exit seems abrupt, as rude as the times.

Do you think a train has feelings? Biggs asks.

Of course not, Little says, playing the straight man, though in truth he likes the idea.

How do you know? Biggs asks, working up to a pronouncement on the consciousness of trains, or something.

It looks wrong, with no caboose, Little chances.

It's like drowning kittens in a barrel, Biggs answers.

How's that?

When you've got an organ that's not pulling its weight you cut it off, Biggs says. *That's the basic law of railroads, my friend,* shooting for something higher.

I like this town, says Little, after a pause.

Biggs looks at him and frowns, pleased for some reason.

How about the river? he asks.

That too.

She's a bitch, Biggs says, *believe me. Chances are she'd break your neck before her tongue was halfway down your throat. With me gone you might just as well. Cools you off, drowning. A town like this is nothing but an oven.*

You've lost me there . . .

You ever had a litter?

I mean about you not being here.

Fact is, there's too many.

Kittens or cabooses?

What is a man during the final seconds, after you've stopped fighting it, and realize you can *breathe under water, just not for very long?*

Little stares at his companion, confused.

You'll never make it, selling, Biggs says.

All a person needs is one true friend, Little says, injured, but sensing his companion's misery.

I'm not really true nor friend. You know that, Biggs says, coming closer to something real.

Don't say that . . .

Are you forgetting the cigarette butts in your drinks? Remember when I put shit in your sandwich? I'd have sold your dog to the Chinks if I'd thought of it.

Where will you go? Little asks, unhappily. This was just Biggs.

Haven't you been listening? I'm headed north, like I should have years ago, when the mud was thick with jobs. You can keep the samples and order books.

Biggs goes to bed with his grievances and he tosses and turns as long as Little is awake to notice. Another train marches past like an army on the move. In the morning Biggs is a stranger, serene in the finality of his decision.

Maybe we'll meet again, he says.

Sure . . .

Someday I'll get it right.

You've got the brains for it.

I'd better get going, don't want this, Biggs says, holding up his thumb, *getting stuck up my ass again.*

That's for sure . . .

My advice is to hit 'em between the eyes, before they know what's coming, sneak in a sale between their confusion and anger, when they're off balance and willing to buy you off.

Little watches him cross the parking lot and slip into the dust grey car. After he's driven away Little sits on the balcony in the sun until he hears the maid next door.

Roused from the perplexing morning he heads into town. On a patch of octagonal war memorial lawn he finds some shade where he opens the sample cases to inventory his three-in-one gadgets and kitchen magnets. A woman walking by sees something she's been searching months for and he makes his first sale. A Mountie stops to chat with him about by-laws and Little sells him a nostril shaver, batteries not included. A couple of slackers attempt some sleight-of-hand, but lose their nerve when they see that Little doesn't seem to care. He has always found people friendly.

He's there for the rest of the day, making the odd sale, drinking water from the public fountain. The take-out guy gives him a free coke with his burger just to be nice. As afternoon progresses, shadows run together like watercolours, and he feels a strand of autumn's long hair, coeval with subtle fragrances of desert, hope.

But at dusk he gets a heavy feeling and a bitter taste in his mouth. He is not glad to see the diffident silhouette lurking nearby—Biggs—or the contradiction of bones walking towards him when he realizes he's been spotted.

I knew it, Little says, in no mood to protect the man's delicate pride.

Come on, let's get something to eat, Biggs says, a don't-over-do-it tone in his voice.

Little takes his time gathering himself off the grass. For most of the day he's been good, peaceful, but now he has to listen to Biggs sawing away like the last cricket on earth, nerve ending against nerve ending. The waitress returns with their water, putting steak knives on napkins. Biggs is like an engine you can't shut off. Normally Little adjusts to it and tries to make a conversation of the bullshit, but he just stares. Biggs rattles recklessly on, having abandoned any attempt at consistency, about terrorists, profitable extinctions, dead children, lawn fertilizers.

The room feels too close, though it isn't the heat or the smoky kitchen. Little feels a weird vertigo, wondering if he's sick. And then he just snaps. Picking up the knife at his elbow he drives it into the table through Biggs' splayed left hand, pinning him there.

Into neutral goes the great truck with reality, coasting free of its gears and constraints. Biggs stares at his spurned flesh and up into Little's surprised face. He calmly moves his fingers, seeing if they work under the circumstances.

He wraps his hand in a napkin and compresses it under his thigh. They study the tip of the blade and ponder the bite in the table, have a quiet meal.

The size of Little's tip makes Biggs grin hopelessly and shake his head, though he says nothing, feeling humbled by this man, the sheer physical bulk of him.

Where we going? he asks, as they cross under the last streetlamp.

Don't worry about it, Little tells him.

They find the path in silence and descend to the riverbank, half a moon showing the way. Sweat evaporating, they cool off beside the constant river, which moves at the impossible pace of the inevitable.

Attack of the
Fifty-Foot Man

Lance was just back from the jungle, still tingling from his first bath in months, sitting in a bar trying to get the taste of wildness out of his mouth. It wasn't working. The women all had spiked hair and strange low-rise jeans. It was like the evolution of a new female body had taken place during the two years he was in Brazil. On his fourth whisky, Jeanie walked over. She was like the others, exoskeleton tightly in place, overconfidence taking the place of being centred.

He studied her, kind of amused, kind of horrified. He bought her several drinks.

Strange weather we're having, he said, though he wasn't making small talk. He'd forgotten how.

Tell me about it. The old man—that is, my dad—is a big insurance freak. It's all he ever talks about. The weather.

You're the first woman I've talked to in . . . months.

Virtual, decidedly.

Learning the ropes with Jeanie meant not asking too many favours, drinking less, being content to watch a lot of TV, and trying to be evasively noncommittal about meeting her family—her parents, her two sisters, the triplets. *Just a thought,* she'd said. But thoughts, like avalanches, pick up everything in their path, pick up the path.

Triplets?

Wanly taking his hand, Jeanie's father, Herbert Waverly, winner of the Top Insurance Standards Award an unprecedented seventeen times, gave Lance a warm squeeze, remarking that a man's handshake was like his castle. Then, breaking down the current payout rates for the loss of a thumb, a finger, he said an entomologist like himself could do well.

Lance hated people, particularly people under nuclear family conditions. He had a turkey dinner flashback—all the stiff, uncomfortable family conversations from his past—and it made him shudder. Man, the lying insect, whose wordy inventions reminded him of a Brazilian termite that builds towers using a mud-like substance that it excretes from its mouth.

Tell me, Dr . . . Lance, Herbert in a more confidential voice, *does your university include coverage for tropical diseases?*

Herbert . . . an elderly woman interrupted them, *won't you introduce me . . .*

She was holding a tray of cookies, which she dismissed Herbert with and benignly proffered a forearm in greeting. It was unusual, and where he lighted like a falcon, her skin was softer than anything he had ever touched, and it lay over a reassuring structure of bone . . .

Lance noticed her lilac scent on his fingers, and she commenced to flirt after the fashion of older ladies with sceptical young men, though he sensed there was something more lurking there.

The occasion was Herbert's sixtieth birthday. Jeanie and her sisters let off steam while Herbert cut his cake and wrenched his dead pan humour into a grimly acted clown. Lance watched with aversion. But you can't observe without being observed. Beatrice was beside him, holding herself up on his arm.

It's lame, she whispered.

Beatrice pulled Lance down closer and put her tongue in the cave of his ear, and he was transported to the seashore.

Jeanie and her sisters were enjoying themselves.

Who wants ice cream on theirs?

Dad?

Delightful, watch that wrist. Rising indemnity for ice cream injuries—

Please, dad . . .

Lance and Beatrice ended up in the kitchen by themselves. She gave him shortbreads that dissolved on his breath, macaroons which imploded. She knit her hands into his on the table like naked puppets thrown together. She moved over beside him on the window seat and found his resolute erection, the tree of his obsessions, the undiscovered cake.

Beatrice was wiping her mouth with her hand when Jeanie thumped into the kitchen followed by her two sisters, like an assembly line of words sounding so alike they cancelled each other out. As if they were on the other side of glass. Then they were gone, the swinging door abandoned to a short-lived gallop.

There's something about you, Lance. It's like you're older than I am.

I'm half your age.

A look in your eye.

I'd been having my suspicions for months.

He started telling her what was on his mind, what precipitated his abandoning his research, leaving the tents and equipment and employees unresolved in the field.

It was that damn Boy Scout manual. I'd picked it up in San Paulo one supply run, from a vendor in a crowded market. I read it at night in camp to escape the heat. It brought back memories of bottle drives in the rain, gave me shivers up the back of the neck. I studied the chapters on semaphore and it was like remembering a lost fucking language.

Then it disappeared. It just wasn't there one night. We were following a foraging colony in those weeks. About a month after the book went missing, I started noticing the ants were marching with bits of paper. I puzzled over this for hours before I knew why I was puzzling over them at all. They were pieces of my Scout manual.

Beatrice nodded, only quietly surprised.

Then the next freaky thing happened. They started swarming on my tent, just on one side. They were doing this for weeks until I realized they were repeating some patterns.

With an unkempt fingernail Lance dug into his scalp and went on with his account.

I tried to imagine how their minds worked, how the collective mind collected. It took time, I admit. I made sketches, took notes. I finally saw it, right there in front of my eyes, they were making the flag positions of semaphore.

My late husband was a signalman in the war.

The ants were relaying something to me across a wide gulf.

What did they say?

. . . 'Be prepared.'

How could you be?

No . . . it was the Boy Scout's motto.

Yes, of course.

I think they meant it as a salutation, a greeting.

What did you do?

I tore my shirt in half and made two flags and started spelling it back a letter at a time, my reply: Long Live the Queen.

What did they say then?

'We didn't know you had language capabilities.'

What? Beatrice was secretly pleased.

Yah . . .

Beatrice spoke passionately about the paths of extinction, remembering the bloody history of cats, the buffalo, the whales.

We must scale down our good intentions, she said without the fervour of youth.

Yes . . . he half agreed.

What Lance didn't want to tell her was how she'd got it

backwards. That it wasn't man studying the ants that was driving another extinction.

They were studying us, he told her. *And we were changing by osmosis, to ant methodologies; inadvertent highways, the need for a man to carry ten times his own weight.*

Later they joined the family in the living room. Their knees stuck like Velcro under the table where a board game was splayed out waiting to be played, but arguments about rules kept cropping up and preventing them from starting.

Herbert got up and closed the curtains and stood there wondering who had opened them. He didn't like being exposed. He peered through the slit at the street.

Though you're covered against everything imaginable, Mr. Waverly, Lance was sensing the man's apprehension and, attributing it to the birthday blues, was only being slightly philosophical, *you're still an insecure guy.*

I enjoy hearing the sound of your voice, Lance, Herbert chided him. *You're a true original, completely uninsurable.*

Can't we have some light for once? Jeanie said, wrenching the dusty things open again.

This had Herbert at a loss, and he just stood there, squinting, like a monument to boredom. In the late afternoon sun an oblique shaft of human skin shone.

What was that hitting? Something shattered the big window. A bullet buzzed past Lance's head, followed by three more unencumbered slugs that tore precisely into Herbert, making him spin like a ceiling fan. The surprise on his face said it all, how now, unexpectedly and so untimely, he must fall, a hollow marionette to the floor.

On the plane south, Lance read an article about gorilla hand ashtrays, and another one about icebergs the size of countries. Beatrice slept in the seat beside him. He didn't know how he was going to get an old woman into the jungle. He didn't know why he had to try. He never knew the reasons for anything he did. Her smile was beatific as he stroked her thinning hair. It had been difficult for her to leave the Waverlys and this he could never understand.

What do you owe them? he asked.

She just smiled sadly, shook her head.

Finally, Lance re-established contact with the subject, the army ants of southern Brazil. Until then he hadn't known what he was going to say. It occurred to him to ask for a few suggestions, how to make things better, like traffic jams. But he thought better of it and asked a more basic question.

What is the meaning of love? spelling it with his arms, speaking it up for Beatrice who was sitting nearby watching.

The ants literally flowed over the side of the tent, drawing with their bodies all the flag positions, Lance following slowly with his pencil.

You can't get drones from a sterile Queen. He read it out.

He thought about it. He didn't know what to say. It threw him. He thought he was the one asking the questions. But at least Beatrice had seen it. He had a witness now. It wasn't all in his head.

Is there such a thing as love, he semaphored again, thinking if he just rephrased the question . . .

But there appeared only randomness on the screen. Did they not understand? He started again, trying other words, there were at least a hundred words for love. Then the ants flowed off the tent and over the ground to Beatrice. They went swarming up her legs and covered her with their little bodies. Maybe they were just trying to help in some way, but they were suffocating her. Beatrice seemed stunned, but strangely resigned. Lance ran around, screaming at them to stop. But it was too late, she was gone. Overwhelmed by a monstrous loneliness, he went on a rampage, tearing at their heart, crushing them under his hands, standing to his full height and bellowing one last anguished cry before they were on him, filling his mouth and ears and eyes and bringing all his strivings to an end.

The Piece

In his mind the piece was located on a field of wheat, where derricks laboured lazily in the distance, and dominating everything was the sky. But that was before he saw the Pacific Ocean and was much improved psychologically by being in Victoria, feeling finally free of something. Adam's prairie senses were raped on the Brentwood shore, though it didn't feel like a crime of violence at the time.

He met a woman in Victoria and moved into the room across the hall. He unpacked his equipment and set up his boxes. Hemlock trees filtered eastern light and it was good; the shadows of leaves made holograms on his table. A busy street ran by on that side, but hidden from view it had some of the qualities of a river. He poured over his sketches, probed for it in his notes, that dialectic of nothing which sometimes he saw and sometimes not. It was four years bringing it off. Now he had to put it up, his blind carpenter's bridge. He had the use of a strip of land next to the bay in exchange for the materials when it came down.

For a few coos the ocean was willing to inspire him. He made pet sounds while he worked. It was a hot summer and hard labour; it was a crash course in physics that required an intricate knowledge of luck. As it grew it shifted and settled into itself, like a spider on acid or a church without walls. Held on wires within were fragments of the old order: a few chairs, an ironing board, a swarm of prisms. But something was beginning to wake up under him, the piece had survived in spite of the tyranny of his intentions.

Incense drifted in the hall between Adam's room and Ruth's. Her music lifted him out of his shores and he experienced the sensation of floating—above her bed, above his conditioning, above his art—suddenly brought back to earth by the shock of the big front door being slammed.

It was heavy and people just didn't think about it. Ruth learned to cope by giving people gentle reminders, offering them a slice of tangerine, a wedge of pomegranate, taping notes in the hall. Her strategy was working too; things had quieted down. Until Bonnie and Clyde—that was what Adam called them—moved in; a girl who, by the looks of it, wasn't old enough to be on her own, and a jumpy inmate with lots of muscle. At first they ignorantly slammed the door like everybody else; but when they realized they were causing people grief, their slamming went from unconscious to launched, thematic, and disrespectful. They disturbed everyone in the building, tailgated the stillness with it, and for some reason regarded this as a kind of ideal state.

Doing art was a science, the science of not knowing how. Nothing helped, neither tears nor guts. Courage was useless, except in surrender: to sacrifice like some grassy virgin, to hear the muse in a different register. Starting with over four years' worth of days, each one like the one before, but in a way different, and there was very little that carried over to make the next one any easier.

About fifty people came to the opening, artists he'd met at the university pub, staff from the art store. They arrived around dusk and parked along the dusty road. When the generator was fired up and Adam threw the big switch they were blinded for a second. But once their eyes had adjusted and their expectations lay dead at their feet they started cheering and clapping. And Ruth was standing there in the middle of it, her arms outstretched in a gesture of glory, his glory. But there was none of that, only the prairie that wasn't, the grand wheat field. The too-bright lights revealed all conventional wrinkles, every unmasked cliché. The stench of kelp on the beach wasn't helping.

Bewildered and sleepless from driving straight through, his old buddies from Winnipeg turned opening night into a sack. They wanted him as they remembered him, and by their glee he saw how reassured they were. It was their most basic ethic, the loyalty of failure. There it was in all its temporal gore, its abacus nakedness, its funded compromise, its executed relationships. The only bridge back to himself, and it was falling short.

His Victoria guests were objective and indifferent. But what of it? Categories are ruts and habits breed the affliction of comfort. It meant nothing. A person wakes up thirty years had and unlearns the house that bullshit built, and all for what? Dreams, body lint. Intention replaces inspiration and self-censor becomes a way of life. But everything authentic comes via his mistakes. The Piece was a naming of this, it was a gallery of his sacrifices, compliments of his future.

While the party raged, Adam shot film, documenting the piece from every inconceivable angle, the subtext showing through, each disparately shimmering nail head. This was the important stage, the point, after all; Adam was a photographer.

The next day a review in *The Times* used words like *vision* and *fresh* to describe the piece. A TV station taped a clip of Adam on the beach and ran it with an "abuse of public money" slant on the arts in general. He was no longer a virgin. He went back to bed.

The following week he finished photographing it even though he was seriously depressed. He needed to play it out professionally, complete his swing. He poured over the prints until his teeth ached. He and his buddies knocked it down and the farmer loaded it onto his pickup truck.

After they took a few loads to the dump, they borrowed some money for gas and said it was time to hit the road. The farmer helped him get the generator into town, but it was too late in the day to return it so they stashed it behind the hedge. About a half hour later Adam noticed it was gone.

He searched between the neighbouring houses, went up and

down the block. He couldn't let it go. He asked Ruth if she had seen or heard anything, but she was busy hanging the prisms he'd given her. He went up to the second floor and knocked on Barney-the-guy-up-stair's door.

Did you see a generator in the yard, behind the hedge?

A generator?

I was using it for my piece.

What piece was that?

My art piece. Adam felt stupid and guilty, he'd neglected to invite Barney.

You're an artist?

Somebody took my generator.

You have a generator?

I rented it.

It's the rental company's problem now. The insurance company's . . . more to the point, I'd imagine.

Adam knew he was right, but he was mad, and he was insulted. Things like this weren't supposed to happen, not here.

Did you talk to the new girl? Barney asked innocently enough, indicating the door across the hall.

Adam hadn't, so he knocked.

Bonnie was jumpy, like an actor who'd forgotten her lines. Behind her was the pig-shaven head of her boyfriend Clyde, much older, but just as poorly rehearsed. Both were clearly guilty of something, if not everything. She was a baby in a size fourteen dress and he was a tube of shit. Adam wanted to laugh, their denials were so comical. He apologized for bothering them and went to his room shaking his head. He made the obligatory call to the police, telling them what he knew, which was, he thought later, probably too much.

Adam did a series of pencil drawings to take his mind off the world of dark buildings with onerous porticos and labial doorways. He set up his projector and showed Barney some of his work from the past, strained oils, wired installations. But Adam was caught in it, in his failure to thrive.

A tense silence had fallen over the house. It was the waiting, waiting for the next jolt from Bonnie and Clyde. Adam went into the hall to yell at them, then he turned up his stereo to block out their dirty mouths. Ruth finally lost it, came over and screamed at him to turn it down. He had intended to stay calm and couldn't believe that he actually hit her. She went still and kind of hovered there. He grabbed his coat and went out.

He walked down Cook Street under the cones of light feeling all grainy, like he was in a film. Ruth was in exile from her dark husband. She feared and lusted too much and when Adam came along what choice did she have? He felt calmer to be around, to have him inside her. A way to fix the door occurred to Adam and so he headed back. He would talk to the landlord if he had to. When he got home, two sedate-looking officers were shining their big lights in his windows. Hovering between them was Ruth.

Adam was living on his credit card, and standing in the liquor store queue he looked startled and guilty. He obsessed over the photographs, tried to see it again, that unnameable inspiration, as he'd seen it before, pushing up through his sketches like a fractured bone. But a huge monolith had overtaken his room and he wondered vaguely what all the strange writing meant.

One night he picked up the phone and dialled a number from his past. The familiar voice of one of his friend's dad on the line:

The boys went camping, he said. *I don't suppose the other campers are too happy about the big screen TV they took with them.*

They took a TV camping?

A bit of over-kill, if you ask me. Say, when you coming by to get your generator?

Adam poured over the piece, through hundreds of black and white prints. The red light on his stereo glowed as he listened to the traffic go by and waited for the hour between three and four when there was a pause in the noise.

The Unbelonging

1. The Last Gig

I buzzed through and climbed the carpeted stairs to the second floor. A woman I found alarmingly beautiful answered and I felt a mutual admiration when she asked me in to wait. It was an apartment with time on its hands, deeply polished, like jade. A tall man with drumsticks poking out of his overnight bag presented himself. It was a tense moment; his hand was damp. I could see that these two were not lovers; there was a sisterly alertness about her, a sadness. She was watching from a window when we climbed into the van.

Driving between Vancouver and Hope the challenge was always in not being hypnotized by the motionless sameness, the endless repeating green. It was a mockery of movement to call this a freeway, goading drivers into proving something, though the faster they went the slower time seemed to drag.

The Fargo van had two seats, driver and one passenger, which meant somebody had to sit on the engine housing facing forward and another had to sit on the back half. It was Chrysler's remarkable slant six that had plunged us on an avalanche of touring, running with enough equipment, amps and guitars, to bury us alive. Up the Fraser Canyon, against the trucks sleepwalking down from the Yellowhead, we moved on into increasingly arid country, trailing the summer behind us, following the knife-scarred face of the river gorge. Descending on Lillooet like a great dusty bird, we circled the hotel a couple of times before it became apparent under its layers.

Through the lobby and into the lounge, where on the far wall portraits of long dead veterans hung. The stage was snug as a cigarette pack once we'd set up our shoulder high amps. I opened my guitar case and released the smell of four years' worth of touring. It was a cascade of memories, of all Mom had done, the calls, the push. Did it have to be. Dare I contemplate foreshadows? No, was loss's quick reply, a twinge of all that was not allowed. Now with mother gone, it was up to us. We were patriots of dust, keepers of the blur.

Memories cluster around smell. Firing Dennis was an attempt to placate the forces of dissolution. It seemed like a good idea at the time, but doesn't bear thinking about now, these new dynamics, this uncertainty of beat, this missing vertebrae.

We had a quick supper in the hotel café and started playing a little after nine. There were few customers as we stamped out Beatles and Stones plugs, normally just a little stale, but that night things were fractured by our fill-in drummer's manic configurations. He was turning out to be our first really and truly useless drummer. Though he was more than useless; he *fought* the beat, damned it. And this was just the first night. We sweated it out, holding the songs together in spite of his musicless careering. By sheer work ethic we managed to get through it.

In the morning I went out early to explore the hills surrounding town and ended up hanging out near the hamburger place. I was escaping my brothers because they grated on my nerves. Down on the flood plain the river seemed married to the forest, the trees locked up in their atoms. It was good to be an alien, to be out of Surrey.

On stage that night the tension was high. We took a few extra breaks to smoke a joint under a hot slab of valley. Normally the band would settle into the flow of whatever it was that swept them along through the landscape of custom. That is, if the locals liked them and kept the rum and cokes coming. But they were playing to nearly no one, a wrung rag, twisted up with the effort to hold the semblance of a beat. We brooded over breaks while the drummer hovered somewhere in one of the booths, beyond our consideration, a scourge.

Dennis, our lost drummer, had become what he was not, the cause of our woes. We sacrificed him to the gods of last ditch, in the great preamble to self-destruct.

In the last set the drummer got so belligerent that Reggie started shouting at him and waving his long finger, which brought the drummer to his feet threatening him with his drumsticks. Reggie unstrapped his bass, dropped off the stage, and hit the floor half-running. He went into the bar and kicked a chair over. Roy and I vainly kept strumming, all snarled up. We gave up too and followed our bass player to the bar, abandoning the stage to the drummer and his drums. We ordered a round of draft and listened to him beating out the last twenty minutes.

I was paid to drum, he said, valiantly, when one of the waitresses asked him to stop.

The next day a humbled silence blanketed the earth, and the 401 was never sleepier. The unbelonging slumped in the passenger seat, impassive. Pulling up in front of his sister's place, I saw her in the window and felt a flush of feeling for her.

Released from the weekend's tension, we headed for home, our will to live renewed, the palpable surrogate heart beating free, and swore we'd never break up.

2. The Summer of Love

I remember now, being slumped on the sofa with my arm around a girl. I hadn't met her before, but it happened so naturally I didn't give it a second thought. Normally I'd be playing my guitar in a corner, going over the three chords, studying a riff. It was neutrality, uncalled for and meaningless. Neither of us tried to analyse it or get to know one another. It wasn't a lack or an overabundance of confidence. It was in somebody's parent's basement. It was a good place to be on a Saturday night. We were a homogeneous group of classless teens. It was the sixties. It was the Summer of Love.

The separate depths of my two brothers and me were evenly backfilled by the move from Nelson. The old man had dumped the last of his business and his pipedreams and got a real job that mostly went to paying off old debts. The new sun burned the exposed roots of a former place and time, and by the third day in our new town we were barely recognizable to each other, though in a way we knew each other better.

That was the day we found the trees. Their roof of green went from the other end of the block to where we were standing. Their thick branches formed a closed circuit, an intricate architecture of inspiration. Abandoned light played high above us in the leaves.

Roy took a cigarette from his pack and put it to his lips.

Give me a butt, I said.

Roy looked at me, held back, troubled, but at the same time pleased. It was played to the music of kindness, the corruption of younger brothers.

He repositioned his glasses on his nose. We were not alone. Leaning against a branch where the hill swelled up underneath it were five other faces.

Roy tapped my arm. I understood and put the proffered cigarette between my lips. Roy twisted a match backwards without tearing it from the book and, with a deft thumb, lit it.

Wanna play tag?

Sure, Roy said, after a thoughtful pause. There was so much to unlearn, convicted of being a fathers' son, knocked into the pitfalls of self-confidence, where deep discontents swept away all magic.

The game lasted all summer and we got to know the trees like streets after dark; and mistakes came with a fall, where gravity increased with accelerating risk. We were learning something, but we didn't know what. Impelled into our skin by the ventriloquist's hand, we were hurtling beyond the ice of Pluto, striking up against something, something that returned us bone to eye. The sarcasm stopped for absolute breathing, cigarettes flared in a distant nebulae.

So there I was with this girl, sunk deep in the sofa, just realizing a whole bunch of things about girls, when somebody pointed a pool cue at me. And a voice at the other end said, *That's him.*

It was the second party in two weeks that Scales and his gang had crashed. The week before, one of them, a big guy named Lund, was kicking one of my friends in the head out in the driveway. *Look at that asshole*, I had proclaimed truthfully. I felt called upon to at least express outrage.

Scales was a gymnast, a fighter. Every time, it was same routine. He'd pick one of us, toy with him for a few hours, finally calling him out. Stench one week, Lucky the next, on some pretext or slight. Poor obedient bastards. *Put 'em up.* How could you not obey that voice? So sure and deep and invincible.

Now he was leaning over me like a deferential storm, *You the guy called my buddy here an asshole? Was that you?* He was polite, reasonable.

I was incapable of thinking on my feet so all I could say was, *Yah, it was me.*

Scales was surprised by my openness, only a little taken aback.

Did you want to do something about it? He put it like he was talking to experience.

His sense of honour demanded that he wait until his opponent took the first shot; that he be fully cognisant of his actions and therefore ready to be flattened. It was important to Scales, honour being the vehicle of his invincibility. But it was also, conversely, his Achilles heel and when I realized this I relaxed.

I shook my head, *No, I don't* . . .

You don't?

No.

You're sure?

Pretty sure.

Scales didn't know what to do.

Okay, if you're sure . . . he took it and went away.

But he kept coming back like it was a sore spot. Each time a little drunker, a little madder, but still unable to arouse me. He called me all kinds of names, but he couldn't call me a coward. This went on until the girl had long gone, had been replaced with my guitar. Scales came back one last time, pointed his finger at me in faked outrage, impotent honour, called me an asshole, then he and his gang left.

I stopped in the middle of the street. A car honked. What that meant was that all these wasted years were not really wasted. I remember this guy telling me one night that he was going to challenge him. He felt it his duty. Ken something . . . he was planning to be a cop. He was sure he was ready.

But Scales was one of the inevitables, another end of some

extreme, a parabola of near misses. He was foreknowledge of life, like discovering a snake in your shoe. He was what you didn't tell your parents about, for fear of making them so powerless they attacked you themselves.

Though I hadn't smoked in years, I dropped into the Hasty Mart for a pack. The point being that I had beaten Scales, the only guy I knew who ever did, and I had never realized it before, not until this, when the last laugh was inevitably his, whether he knew it or not. My wife just left me you see, for a guy whose older brother used to be a member of Scale's gang. The guy that ratted that time.

I strip off the cellophane, light my first one, amazed. Yes, I remember the challenger who was going to be a cop. Ken, he was sitting there after the fight, telling everyone who went in—bragging almost—that he was beaten fair and square. He was chagrined, but not destroyed. In a way he looked older, through some portal. Glad.

3. Kitten

The university building was situated halfway down the bank of the Old Man River coulee. A refuge from body blow dust storms and allegorical sheets of ice, the Erickson Building was meant to inspire, yet it resembled a coffin exposed by successive hundred-year floods. You could see it from the opposite rim of the canyon where a small house jutted from the edge, where, just beyond, the Great Plains crouched under a cavernous sky, and a sinuous breeze was always pacing.

It was autumn when Barney and Bell finally unpacked. The first month and a half in the Coaldale Motel was behind them. She quickly found work with her bank and Barney passed the days until his classes started, exploring Indian Battle Park and doing pastels of the prairie autumn. The decision to move happened through a series of small moments: would the university accept him, how was the town for bands, each acting like a switch, directing their growth here, of all places. Leaving B.C.

was like shedding something, it was liberating to have the placenta of the too familiar off his shoulders.

And as it turned out, being married wasn't so difficult. Bell's beauty continued to grow on him and her ease with people supported his introverted talents. She brought out his potential and bore his passions loyally. They were buddies and lovers and a good thing for each other. Though thoughts that she was no stunner lingered at a distance. He hated when they came, with their aftertaste of fear.

Lethbridge had a trestle, the longest in the world. Its foundation girders spanned the coolie, ignoring the river like an old woman in black lace tiptoeing over the park. Coming into town that first time on their honeymoon, it was remarkable, a tectonic suture. A train floated overhead like a line of geese.

Bivouacked on the edge of the gorge was the city of forty thousand. By way of a panoramic view, the sky was about all it had. An imported plan created unforeseen tunnels and ghosty corners the wind took a special interest in, known for knocking old ladies off their feet. It whipped Barney's long hair into his eyes, while Hutterite ladies skimmed the bright beige landscape like bashful black sails. It was exciting for the newlyweds, exceptional. The man-eating weather was never far off, but they were free of that stalker known as the past.

A few weeks before the wedding, his cold feet hard-pressed the truth. So flat were the words, Bell was struck dumb. *I wish I could see other women.* It was a moment of candour, an openness, though inappropriate and unkind. He could offer no way back, being only half-aware he'd said it, leaving Bell to haggle with her expectations, wondering and back-peddling right up to the night before. On the big day, there it was between them: a burden, like a mongoloid son. Dearly beloved, the guests were oblivious, though the sandwiched-between-funerals minister seemed to know Barney was guilty of something. And they all felt better with the deed done, though it took a few days into the honeymoon for it to stop bothering Bell. It was no more than a grain of sand she confessed, smiling, her skin regaining its nacre blush.

The woman who ran the Coaldale Motel had a scar from one side of her throat to the other. She communicated in grunts and barks and got by on her looks. It was the hottest summer in years and big sweaty insects crawled into the unspoonable heat with them, the smells of evening seeping from their neighbours' gloomy hideouts. Coming back from a late-night practice, Barney found Bell in a heap on the floor. Why hadn't someone prepared him for this? He thought the world must have ended. He kissed her tears. How could she not know from that? Symbols and opposites were all he had to negotiate the unfamiliar, the tender. She said she was waiting for the axe to fall, wondering when he was going to have an affair. He said he was happy with the way things were turning out. She said how cold his hands were and awkwardly warmed them under her arms.

The band he was rehearsing with started playing regularly. Combined with what he got for teaching guitar he was bringing in nearly as much as Bell. Twenty students a week kept him busy from mid-afternoon 'til early evening. It was like everything was prearranged by fate. With an hour to spare, he grabbed a sub and drove to the gig, his guitar and amp in the back seat. They started at nine and stopped at one in the morning. He was at home in bed with Bell by three at the latest. She got up before him and he had the morning and early afternoon house to himself, his first scheduled student wasn't until three-thirty. He sacrificed the university classes, with their unreadable handouts and pathetic faculty. What had once seemed so essential—making up for something he could barely define—had lost some of its poignancy. Things were going well, you could say. As well as a funny small house all to themselves, they had adopted a kitten and given it a clever name.

The band was called Spider and it consisted of a blues clavinet player, a three-fingered bassist, and a bi-polar chick singer named Tara. Though formally he knew little, Barney fit in his contraption of notes, his solos shaped by adaptation and mistake. They played a lot of bars and the bars all had dance floors and everyone drank and the dancers followed Barney's driving, varying rhythm.

The fact that he was married and expressly happy about it didn't stop Tara Likely from flooding her banks over him, though she eased off when she heard his brother, Reggie, was planning a visit. It was to be brief, if it happened at all, as visits were with his capricious younger brother. Barney was only a year older, though this gave him the right of absolute power over

Reggie, but only until their early teens when they discovered music and that Reggie was better at it. Barney's domineering ways came to an end as Reggie rose to a position of ascendancy. But former slaves make for conflicted masters and the band came apart at the seams. Since going separate ways, Reggie's been on the road continuously, playing in a metal band with aspirations well past their due date. It broke up on the road somewhere between painful and embarrassing and Reggie rolled into town like a loose hubcap. He wasn't even sure he felt like staying the night, manic for the coast, but Barney pulled rank and gave him a second beer.

Spider was playing at the Marquis that night and Tara Likely was in particularly good form. That's what Barney thought, though Reggie said he wasn't impressed with the way she handled certain phrasings. A bit too showy, he said. Flip. She was a hard person to see with all the bright matter orbiting, and waited until the second break to sit down with them. Reggie never saw what hit him. She got hold of a few of his loose ends and both were quickly tangled up. He didn't need the spare bed, as it turned out; he'd found a place to crash.

Kitten happened to go missing on the same weekend Bell was away. Anxious to tell her the story, Barney rehearsed it driving to the airport. How it was gone for two days and then turned up in the hedge bloodied and shivering with terror. Something had tried to eat it, and being a sheltered cat until then, it was stricken, disillusioned big time. Something was bothering Bell though. Barney could see it right away, from where he waited on the other side of the metal detectors. He reversed the plot, putting the happy outcome first, anticipating her emotions, lest she express one, which Barney didn't like, because when she did it was like a fissure in the framework opened up. But she was aloof and distracted until they were home, where she told him about some jerk that had invited her to his room. Though she had refused, she needed to tell Barney about it, to confess to something, to warn him. A kind of tit for tat, and though he nodded to show he understood, he didn't really.

Bell had found the cat through an ad at the laundromat and that it was a peculiar cat was obvious from the first. It opened doors it shouldn't have been able to. It watched Barney, almost pitying him. Bell told him he was paranoid, but he swore there was something else. From Kitten's perspective, something was wrong with these wasteful, worried—these inferior, furless, justifiers who were always constructing philosophic explanations for what they did not see. Plain as night, a reversal was stalking Barney, getting ready to unlock its jaw. Bell was trying to squeeze into one cookie-cutter after another, the banana diet, the strawberry daiquiri.

Reggie smiled when he heard they were planning to move back to B.C., laughing like he'd just heard the funniest joke ever and was delighted with himself for having thought of it. Barney and Bell hadn't expected to stay in Lethbridge forever, settling wasn't in Barney's vocabulary. And only someone who's never lived in B.C. wouldn't understand the pressure it puts on you to return. The summers, the beaches, the chemical highs, Chinese lanterns in a tongue-warm breeze, so good the first time, though hard to recapture. It was a place where mountains could collapse like a drunk on the steps. Kitten was watchful, nervous. And as Barney well knew, the best way to preserve something was to destroy it. Barney and Bell would move on to a more familiar river and its memorized curves. They toyed with the idea like foreplay. The narcotic of optimism, when every action was a reaction to what is spurning you on. Success would follow them, for surely its form was transportable to any old host. The shimmering lake of potential, the take-no-prisoners personality of rivers, the beast of too damn bad.

Bell thought Barney was different after Reggie joined Spider, replacing Tara as their vocalist when she got pregnant. Bell had learned to surrender to his right-angle turns, feeling dizzy a lot of the time. He was so credulous that she wanted to believe in him, though she was nervous too of his tentative revisions and half-serious considerations. To Kitten, neither of them looked up from their world of shadows, constantly colliding with the thought that they're special. Their best friends, Lauren and Lucky, knew of a house available and Lucky's band needed a guitarist.

Barney drove the three ton, loosely piled with their clapboard belongings. Bell drove the VW bug out front by a few car lengths. He could see the cat, abated with Valium, pressed against the back window. It was a winter day and they drove out of town past the trestle, snapping a few pictures of it from the cab to make up for the ones he'd meant to shoot before, during all the chances he'd had. But it was black and remote against an unmoving winter sky.

Exhausted from the conniving icy roads, turning into the rural darkness, his destination vanished. They were almost there, tires squeaking on the snow around one corner and then another. What was this for? Whose life did this move make sense in? He couldn't remember if he had reasons. The river, yes, he'd come for the river, for those pure moments the four of them cavorted like seals; for Lauren, her perplexing perfections, for Lucky, his perplexing flaws. At the end of the street they launched inner tubes and an hour later were several years happier. It took them east and then straight back like the outline of a woman's slightly parted legs.

They pulled up on the street outside their new house. The river was frozen. Barney stepped out of the cab to the astringent smell of wood smoke. Bewilderingly brave, Bell shivered beside the car, Kitten's breath clouding the rear window. It was coming to him, dawning, as they say. He didn't mean this. It was just a way to hear himself think, a game. The rewind button in his brain, he was going to find it. He listened for morning to fabricate, for him to realize it was just a nightmare, for that feeling of reprieve. Lucky had spent the past two days shovelling their driveway and expected some appreciation, though all Barney felt was murdered.

Lucky's band was run by a thick bass player who needed

everyone to be spinning their tops in the same direction as he. When Lucky told him about Barney he was enthusiastic, though once face-to-face they were on different hemispheres, bitter as aspirin. The months deepened and natural light was sacrificed for a piddling heat the closed curtains provided. Bell did her best to cope with Barney's bewildering decline, spending more time up the street with Lucky and Lauren, glad to be at the bank working instead of at home. By the time spring recaptured the small town, Barney was in the throws of a breakdown and the corrupted retreating snow laid bare an urgent need for him to find something to do. Never trained for the business world, for the gizmo factories and bloody parachutes, it all seemed a mockery, and he felt startlingly unprepared for it. The Okanagan had been in a recession since who knows when, making it a bad place to start from scratch.

Lucky and Barney wore thin on each other pretty quick, quickly as these things go. Bell and Lauren said nothing about the all-night sessions, the perpetual discussions the two of them had, their low frequency beating out a misplaced code. When the four of them played cards, Barney got so stoned he couldn't speak, and Lucky regularly tumbled down the basement stairs. Look at them, Kitten thinks and turns away, they're as dignified as a dog chasing its ass. Through the cat door, outside for some clean air. Up onto the shed roof, eyes shining with galaxies. But no, Murphy was out, the bane of the old tom up the street, its chillingly human eyes.

They moved again, and this time the cat didn't need Valium. It was greener pastures for Smitten Kitten. Coming into Victoria she was perched at Bell's shoulder, cruising along the rocky shore, alert to the ocean's adumbrations of doom. The gardens were inspired, monster rhododendrons swallowed whole city blocks. They moved into a two-level prefab in the sticks and rattled around like marbles in a can. Barney found a minimum wage preoccupation; apparently he had acquired a trade. Illuminated signs were the future.

He made shameful drunken passes at Bell's friends, because literature and music were apparently against marriage. Divorce had more resonance, more symbolic purity. It was common knowledge that first marriages didn't work. Twice Barney attempted to break it off, point blank range, no point discussing it. And twice Bell absorbed and dispersed the energy of his escapes with some kind of space-age material only women weave, softening him to her bloom once again. Panicked herself, in some vague and autonomic pilot, she told him she wanted a baby. Great matters decided, as in a dream; once upon a time distilled to a single drop of now or never.

A can of pears was all the proof Barney needed. Her denial that anything was out of the ordinary made it conclusive. The dead rabbit was a formality. Kitten decided it was time to leave. What a burden they'd become, these busy blind. Their service would no longer be required. The rural woods and template backyards were a happier lot. Just one misstep under a pale sky was all it would take. Every day was her last, that month she dined on the living. Put off at first by their throes and unanswerable prayers, she grew to savour it. Mice, following their underground vibrations; birds, by their anxious warnings. She liked her dinner terrified, it brought out the flavour of the meat.

Lucky and Lauren were in town when Bell got word from her doctor. They happened to pick her up from work that day and she couldn't keep it to herself. They stopped at the liquor store on the way home for champagne.

He pulled it off flawlessly, shooting the spare room door with one frantic cork. He named the tyke Ace, laughed at everybody's jokes, reassuring them that everything was fine, though Bell knew in his mind he was already packed and gone. Even though it would be pure folly for any man to run from a pregnant wife, Bell knew he was no coward, and that this was going to show him.

Barney saw a calico splotch on the highway. It seemed more like an article of clothing than a psychotic pussycat. Barney didn't tell Bell because Bell was gone. And it had no meaning to the nineteen-year-old violinist whose precise fingers were intertwined with his on the beer-wet table.

You've ruined my life, Bell had choked out, kicking him as hard as she could, humiliating him with its sheer intention to inflict. She had just woken up and there was Barney's cold news. He just spilled it and she was gone with the car.

Barney clung to a fistful of daffodils and mounted his new girlfriend's foyer, nearly doubled over with another aftershock, even though it had been a week since Bell left. They come on him with crushing force, welling up from his organs, from his identifications. But he was okay, he had no rights. He was the bastard, but he would ring again. That was her voice, who the flowers were for, but she wouldn't buzz him in. There on the sidewalk, six floors down, he wrestled with a gargoyle's name.

What was it, my plum, forget what you were going to say? May it please the court, he did what he thought he was supposed to. He got out of everyone's way.

4. The Five-Hundred-Year-Old Man

Cottonwood Lake was the deepest lake in the world, with marlin-sized trout and worms a quarter mile long. It was where the Nazis had a submarine base and how aliens crossed interstellar space. It was the size of a few football fields, yet deeper than Erie or Loch Ness. It took years for air bubbles to wobble bottom up from the ooze towards the light.

When I asked my brother to teach me about pools he told me to simply look. I saw him whispering to the quicksilver, and by his listening I saw it replied. I had to be content to see my tackle rise unsnagged from the deadheads while Roy was a puppeteer with a fly.

Early evening's softened sun shone through a cotton shift the lake was wearing, revealing mother of pearl insects dancing above a brief chilly mirror.

In dung pastures, we elbowed summer and gathered our

bikes under crab apple trees. Older brothers had a purpose, to expose the Sisyphus wheels and the slag heaps; while an uncle would have spared you, and a father was just part of the conspiracy to keep things hidden.

When my brother told me about the five-hundred-year-old man, I had no doubt. A scrupulous child sees intangibles as the highest court in the land. On the shale side of inaccessible, just below dark, shivers ossified. My brother saw the five-hundred-year-old man throwing something into the lake.

In a hundred years the population of Nelson hadn't changed, while cities elsewhere had metastasized like crazy. Though it wasn't through lack of trying, turning out in feral scores every category of runny-nosed Oedipus.

The century had wars to blame for the missing. During the thirties it was the winds. The forties had crosses numerous as locusts, and during the fifties they came in the night for the Doukhobor babies and the gifted cripples, taken from their mother's warm kitchens, skinned of consolation, and left for alive somewhere else. How it must have delighted him, B.C., where he could weave in his loose ends, where everything was so maintained, and air raid sirens frowned down but wouldn't be heard over the wailing of the Russian bombers floating above the schoolyards.

Fishing Cottonwood Creek, we found a shelter once, a patch of dry in the shape of a lanky foetus. Maybe it was his. The stories came back to me over the years, bobbing to the surface with a splash. Only by his Frankenstein self did the average child come to know himself, that he was hunted for the good of man. The exiled sons of jealous fathers let the five-hundred-year-old man lure them away, knowing he would cook them until their flesh came away from their bones and a thin film of fragrant oil floated on the surface.

•

And the years didn't occur consecutive; rather they came stacked like chicken cages on the back of a truck, privacy not all it might have been. In a blue moon we fished, in the cracks between decades, during good rain and bad. Silver hair now white, neither of us bothering much with our mouths.

We made our way up the rusting sluice, lost to the rest, the paper chapels, the seismograph hills. It hit me that maybe lies weren't so untrue, that maybe it's not the story that matters. Somehow you survive, punch-drunk, staggering in swarms of bees. From morning to morning we carve old words in stone, pay the upkeep on our cages. And the light, crazy new versions appear; you have to close your eyes to see anything. But the body language of fishing eludes, scared of the jumping heart, mistaking the strange noise of ecstasy for dread.

about the author

Robert Strandquist's work has appeared in *subTerrain, The Capilano Review, Prairie Fire, Fiddlehead, Grain,* and *Event.* Mr. Strandquist has a MFA from the University of British Columbia and has received several writing awards, including a Canadian Authors' Association award for poetry. He grew up in Nelson, B.C. and now resides in Vancouver.